Praise for *Our Little Secret*

NATIONAL BESTSELLER

Winner of the Douglas Kennedy Prize for Best Foreign Thriller

Finalist for the Kobo Emerging Writer Prize

Finalist for the Arthur Ellis Best First Crime Novel Award

"A cracking read. . . . Builds to a deliciously dark conclusion."

Ruth Ware, #1 *New York Times* bestselling author of *The Woman in Cabin 10*

"One of the best grip-lit titles of the year. . . . The writing is supremely seductive. Nay draws the reader in with compelling characters, deliciously dark themes, clever turns of phrase, and heightened levels of suspense. Nay's psychological thriller will have readers clamoring for more."

Toronto Star

"Roz Nay's addictive debut proves that dark secrets of the past cannot be forgotten."

Us Weekly

"*Our Little Secret* superficially resembles Paula Hawkins's *The Girl on a Train* and similar psychological thrillers that have stormed the bestseller lists in the last decade. But Nay's work transcends the subgenre. The plot is more textured and heartbreaking, and her prose contains startling turns of phrase that reveal the soul of a poet."

The Washington Post

"A memorably twisted love story."

Entertainment Weekly

"Lures readers down a dark and tangled path that explores the aftereffects of lost first loves. A gripping addition to the psych thriller world."

Mary Kubica, *New York Times* bestselling author of *The Good Girl*

"A guaranteed good read. . . . You're likely to read it in one breathless sitting."

The Globe and Mail

"A sneaky-smart, charismatic debut."

Booklist (Starred Review)

"A clever and addictive read that had me enthralled from the first chapter all the way to the shocking twist that left me breathless. Roz Nay is going to be a name we hear a lot of in the future."

Chevy Stevens, bestselling author of *Still Missing*

"Fans of Paula Hawkins and Ruth Ware will devour this twisty psychological thriller. Nay has expertly crafted a narrative that has the potential to veer in several directions, keeping the readers enthralled and guessing until the end."

Library Journal (Starred Review)

"Keeps readers enthralled with prose that's at once lyrical and incisive."

Shelf Awareness

"Roz Nay shows how the past is never truly past, and can be darker than we guess, especially when it comes to first loves. A most promising debut."

Andrew Pyper, bestselling author of
The Demonologist and *The Homecoming*

"A gripping and unsettling story that left me guessing until the very end."

B. A. Paris, author of *Behind Closed Doors*

"The breadcrumbs Nay expertly leaves behind reveal a dark truth you won't see coming. Ruth Ware fans will love this compulsive, impossible-to-put-down novel!"

Karma Brown, bestselling author of
The Life Lucy Knew

"Nay expertly spins an insidiously clever web, perfectly capturing the soaring heights and crushing lows of first love and how the loss of that love can make even the sanest people a little crazy. Carve out some time for this riveting, one-sitting read."

Kirkus Reviews

Turn to the back for a sneak peek at Roz Nay's next novel

HURRY HOME

Coming to bookstores Summer 2020

OUR LITTLE

SECRET

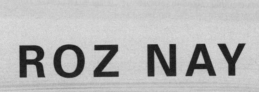

ROZ NAY

Published by Simon & Schuster
New York   London   Toronto   Sydney   New Delhi

SIMON &
SCHUSTER
CANADA

Simon & Schuster Canada
A Division of Simon & Schuster, Inc.
166 King Street East, Suite 300
Toronto, Ontario M5A 1J3

This Simon & Schuster Canada edition April 2020

SIMON & SCHUSTER CANADA and colophon are trademarks of Simon & Schuster, Inc.

For information about special discounts for bulk purchases, please contact Simon & Schuster Special Sales at 1-800-268-3216 or CustomerService@simonandschuster.ca.

Interior design by Lewelin Polanco

Manufactured in the United States of America

10 9 8 7 6 5 4 3 2

ISBN 978-1-9821-0520-4
ISBN 978-1-5011-4280-2 (pbk)
ISBN 978-1-5011-4286-4 (ebook)

For Clint
and all the lies he doesn't tell

OUR LITTLE
SECRET

FRIDAY

chapter

1

I've been in the police station all morning while they ask me questions about Saskia. Every hour the cops come to me, one after another, with a new pad of paper and a full cup of coffee. They must pass off the same brain at the door when they leave, hand it over like an Olympic baton, because not one of them strays from the script. *Do you know the woman well? Can you speculate on where she's gone? Are you upset? Angry? How do you feel about Mr. Parker? Would you consider your relationship with him to be particularly . . . close?* Always a pause before the adjective.

That's the thing: they sound like they're asking about Saskia, but all roads lead to Mr. Parker and me. The police want to know if I'm in love with him, and they ask it like it's the simplest explanation rather than the most complicated. My definition of love is nothing like theirs, though. Language can't link us anymore: somewhere along the way, the important words got emptied and dulled, bandied around until they lost all electricity. Honestly, I don't think they know what they're asking.

Mr. Parker. It's funny to hear his name that way; to me he's HP and he always will be. For the hours I've sat in this room with cold-faced interviewers who don't know me, it's him I miss the most. I've done nothing wrong and until I know what's happened, I'm saying nothing. Cross my heart and hope to die, stick a needle in my eye, I'd tell the whole truth and nothing but the truth, but it's like they're trying to solve a puzzle by fix-ating on one piece, as if it might change shape for them if they prod at it for long enough with their chimpy thumbs. They sit with their heads down, anticipating my answers and writing them in before the words are even mine. I wonder if it matters what I tell them.

The walls in this room merge with the floors in a sheen of polish: you can't tell where one ends and the other begins. It's as if no living creature ever spent time in here. The sole sign of humanity is on the wall to my left: one small line of graffiti written in fervent black capitals. THE URGE TO DESTROY IS CREATIVE. I've looked at it all morning, and it makes me worry about who sat here before me and what they were up to.

The only furniture in the room is a chrome table with four chairs, all the legs stubbed with rubber to avoid scarring the floor. Above the door a clock with a beige face judders its long hand through the seconds. In the top-left corner is a video camera. The red light winks at me. There's one window up high to my right, but the glass doesn't open. The long, thin pane glints like a reptile tank in a pet store. The police station parking lot must be out there. I often hear car doors banging.

There are other interview rooms on this corridor—I'm sure of it, because the air sucks in like a gasp every time the police officers open a door. Who's being questioned in those rooms? I can't be the only one they've brought in.

At noon they send in a fresh recruit. This one is dressed in a suit with a name badge clipped on his right pocket.

"Hello, Angela." J. Novak studies the clipboard on his lap.

He writes the time in twenty-four-hour digits and fills out his name on the dotted line. J for James? John? Jekyll? He's shaved his sideburns so that his hair cuts a strange line over the tops of his ears.

"How are you feeling this morning?" He clears his throat, and his Adam's apple bobs. "I'm Detective Novak. I've been asked to take the lead because I specialize in homicide cases." He exhales, an apology for his talents. "Here, I brought you water and food." He holds out a generic bottle of water and two granola bars. When I don't respond, he places them gently on the table. "Look, we really need you to talk to us, to help us find Saskia. If you could just fill in the blanks, we can close your file." Detective Novak's pen drums against the clipboard in a measured pulse. The top is chewed into a dented peak.

"I have a question." My voice bounces around the vinyl walls. Novak's dark eyebrows shoot up. He puts his pen down.

"Fire away," he says, like we're just hanging out over lattes.

"Do you *really* want to know what happened?" My voice is a tiny husk. It's the only question anyone should ever need to ask.

Novak smiles, a tight line on his lips, and pulls the sleeves of his jacket lower to cover his shirt cuffs. He puts both palms flat on each side of his paper, the pen horizontal at the top like a spoon at a place setting. He is waiting to be fed.

My mother always taught me not to ask questions you don't want answers to. *Mind your manners, Angela. You're so nosy, so grabby. You're so needy; have I taught you nothing about being a lady?* Twenty years I lived with my parents and we never really talked about anything. We were just moles fumbling along in the same dark tunnel.

These days when all three of us meet, we blink at each other in the bright surprise of my adulthood and flounder for a point of reference. But if I think about it now, maybe my mother was right. In among all her competitive disapproval lay a gristly knuckle of truth: don't ask what you don't want to know.

Detective Novak, I don't trust your curiosity.

I prod my forefinger on the chrome of the table, leaving a smeared fingerprint. "I'll tell you all I can, on two conditions."

He waits.

"I know Saskia. I know what she's like. Is it really true she's been missing since last night?"

He nods.

"I want to know why you think it's a homicide case. She might have just wandered off. Maybe she flew back to wherever she came from."

He pauses, frowning. "At this point we're considering all possibilities."

"Good, because you shouldn't rule anything out. You don't know what people are capable of."

That one he writes down. I wait for him to finish, the full stop at the end of his line carefully pressed. He lifts his head. "What's your other condition?"

"My what?"

"You said there were two conditions."

"Oh, I don't want to talk about Saskia the whole time."

Novak's teeth are flat at the front, four of them in a row. "She's kind of the main event."

A black thread dangles from the hem of my shirt. I coil it around and around my forefinger until the skin at the tip shrieks purple. "I'm sorry to break it to you, Detective, but the story I have for you isn't really about her.

There's a skill to finding where a tale truly begins, and trust me, there was action long before there was Saskia." I yank the thread free, roll it into a tiny ball and launch it to the floor.

"Start wherever you like, Angela. I'm a captive audience."

We study each other.

"Am I a suspect, Detective Novak?"

He uncrosses and crosses his long legs. "Like I say, the investigation's ongoing. At this stage we're just filling in the blanks. We don't know for sure what we're looking at. And you're helping us form a . . ." He cups his hands as if around clay. ". . . a clearer picture."

"I doubt I can help. I know HP more than I do Saskia, and most of what I can tell you is a decade old."

His mouth smiles but his eyes don't. "Just tell me what you know."

I shrug. "Okay, here we go."

So, Detective Novak, can we talk about me for a change? In my experience, it's not a subject that gets much forum and I have a lot to say. It might even end up being cathartic. Thank you—I'll take it from that slight incline of your head that you'll let me offload for a while, whether or not you have a choice.

Let's go way back and begin with how my parents

moved a lot. My mom and dad bonded over their rest-lessness and rushed to get married in it. They met as amateur actors in a play and once they had me, we were up and moving every three years as if our life was a stage production they thought they were touring. One of my earliest memories is of being four, maybe, and in the middle of cutting out a picture of a turkey from the grocery-store coupons. My fat little hands were squashed right into the scissor handles, cutting in a curve, when my mom started jangling her keys next to my head and telling me we had to go, right now, baby, out the door, let's go. Right now, leave that, just *leave it*. She yanked the scissors out of my hand and stood over me while I struggled to find my shoes.

I went through my whole childhood like that. Ready to be yanked away.

The moves were career-related for my father—he's always been a man with one eye on the success ladder, although if you ask me he must have been climbing the rungs in his slipperiest socks. *Ad astra per aspera, Angela—to the stars the hard way.* It was tiring watch-ing him. Still, my mother was happy to accompany him as long as each step felt like a social climb. There was a giddiness to their choices in those early years, a strange excitement. *Darling, just imagine!* Each time they left a place, my parents must have believed they were on their way to somewhere they might actually be happy.

Moving when you're fifteen is terrifying. It's not fun, it's not an adventure, it's not a wild ride to wonderful things, baby. In Grade 9 I said good-bye to my friends and watched them fade away from me even while I was still standing there. When people get older, they're supposed to cope better with separation, but I don't know whether that's true. Are we honestly meant to believe the important ones will stay with us wherever we go?

We drove three hours northwest to Cove, Vermont, in the fall just as Grade 10 began. You probably love this town to death and all, Detective Novak, you're probably New England born and bred; but I've got to tell you, the first time we drove down Main and Oak Streets it looked like we'd arrived in the sister town of somewhere more exciting, the kind of place you move to because the housing's cheaper. Sure, Vermont is all covered bridges and maple-candy shops, and life is like the lid of a Christmas cake tin, but when we drove into Cove town center, there was a hardware store, a scattering of bars with faded HAPPY HOUR banners over their doorways and a Tastee Delite with a hand-scrawled sign in the front window that read GET YOU'RE POPSICLES NEXT JULY, YOUR AMAZING—I swore I'd never eat there. The town's curling rink looked like a Cold War bomb shelter from the outside, and the riveted metal of the roof clanged with raindrops as we drove by with the car windows down.

9

The house we bought was sad and gray and looked hunched like it was coughing. There was a shoe in the driveway. In the middle of the front lawn was an iron stake driven deep into the dirt, with a rusted chain on the grass.

"Dog owners." My mother shuddered to my father. "David, we'll need a commercial cleaner."

Do you like living in a town of only four thousand people, Detective Novak? Isn't it a cozy little community? Dad knew and liked the principal of the high school and felt the move to a smaller place would somehow benefit my chances of getting into a good college. *It's all about class sizes, my dear. Teacher–student ratio. Let's shoot for the Ivy Leagues.* He took a job at the Cove Municipal Library, giving up his research post at the Museum of Fine Arts in Boston because he had become obsessed with my education. Either he'd lost the trail of his own success and was now starting to sniff out mine, or else he was trying to relive his glorious Yale days where he aced his Classical Civilization class and spent heady afternoons reading *The Iliad* under the shade of the maples. I never wanted to leave the city. Small towns are a soap opera: you're either acting or you're watching.

I went to Lakeside High, although I'm sure you already know that. It was a flat-roofed brick building with basketball hoops out front that had long ago lost their netting. The first day in that school my palms smelled tinny and sour from gripping the iron hand-rails that led up to the front entrance. The locker they gave me still had stickers in it from the kid before—rainbows that were plastic and puffy and crinkled when you pressed them. I pried them all off with my thumbnail.

At every school I attended, gym teachers sighed when they saw me coming, and Lakeside High was no different. At the end of gym on that first Monday, I went to change back into my regular clothes and there were knots in the ends of my pants, pulled so tight that two people must have put their full weight into the job. I couldn't tease the knots apart. By the time I sat down in defeat, the locker room had emptied.

"Angela, is it?" The teacher came in with her class list clasped to her rock-hard chest. "Angela Petit-jean?" She said it like this—*pettitt-gene*. Not much of a linguist. "What's happening here?" She wore a polo shirt with all the buttons done up, and her bangs were hair-sprayed to one side. "Who did this? Holy smokers, they put some effort into it." As she spoke, she grunted and ground her fingers into the knots, easing them loose. "Okay—here. Now, pick up the pace! You'll be late to your next class."

My pants had a crimped hemline for the rest of the day, like an '80s disco look. I knew who did it; I knew

11

right away because two girls followed me down the hallway laughing when I emerged from the gym. And they were everywhere: waiting outside the washroom, behind me in the lineup for lunch and three lockers down, leaning against the wall while I tried to get my books organized for English class. The taller one wore dark-purple nail polish and a T-shirt that showed her belly button. Pierced. The other girl dressed identically, even down to the love-heart laces in her sneakers. What is it about teenage girls that makes them impossible to tell apart? I thought it was all in the styling, the makeup, the cloning of boy-band music and favorite movies. Now I realize what bonds and homogenizes them: panic.

Haven't you noticed, Detective Novak? Girls of fourteen move together in a band of cruelty, always searching for somebody to terrorize as long as it keeps the spotlight off them. They'll hunt in twos or more because if you're standing alongside the sniper, it's unlikely you'll be the one in the scope.

"You're new, aren't you?" the tall one said. "Yeah, we're not really okay with that." They giggled. "We like to be asked before things change."

I didn't say anything back, but I remember reaching as far into my locker as I could, short of climbing in there and shutting the door.

"What's with your pants?"

Just then a voice stopped them.

"Back up there, sisters."

I peeped around the edge of my locker and saw a tall boy a few doors down. He was about fifteen, olive-skinned, blond, with a sleeveless Metallica T-shirt that showed the early bump of deltoids. He wore sand-blasted beads around his neck and a navy baseball cap with a D on the front.

"Oh, hey, HP." Girl number one shook back her bangs.

"Oh, hey," Girl number two echoed. "Where'd you come from?" She stretched gum from her mouth and twirled the glistening loop with a forefinger.

"Swim practice." He slammed his locker door and walked towards me.

I think my head tried to turtle down into my shell in that moment as I stood there in my crinkly pants, wide-eyed, holding my English textbook.

"Come on," he said. "I'll walk you to class."

This is where the story begins. Grade 10, eleven years ago. Mark it on your sheet, Detective Novak. I'm telling this like it's the beginning of a love story; I'm catering to your needs as a listener. But we both know that's not where the narrative's heading, right? I mean, it's bound to get much darker—why else would I be telling it in a police interview room? I like that you're humoring me and letting me steer the ship for a minute. Of course, you might feel I'm not cutting to the chase quickly enough, the way you're tapping your toe on the linoleum like that; but to be fair, if the chase is a murder, then why am I even here? You want me to just keep going? Okay, whatever you say.

HP and I started down deserted hallways, him scuffing an empty raisin packet along the floor every fifth step. I hadn't walked beside many boys before—it was all I could do to sneak a glance at the side of his smooth face. A small curve of hair kicked up from under his hat.

"Don't let Christie Burbank work you over. She's got nothin'. Just call her Spermbank, that'll slow her down." He stopped to tie the lace of his high-top. "And the other one's Danielle Moyzen. I call her Moistbum." His face craned up towards me. "What's your name, anyway?"

"I'm scared to tell you," I said, and he laughed.

When he stood up, he pulled the top of my English book down from where I held it clenched against me.

"Angela Petitjean," he said, properly, reading the label on the front. "English Ten. Okay, you're in here." He opened the classroom door for me. As I walked through it, he added, "See you around, Little John."

It was the only class of the day I went into smiling.

He walked me home, too. It turned out he lived a block up from me in a house with a huge birch tree out front. I was ahead of him, trudging along in my gray Converses, when I heard footsteps catching up with me. I turned and there was HP, running with his thumbs hooked under the straps of his skull-embossed backpack.

"Hey," he said.

"Hey."

We walked in silence as I racked my brain for a conversation to have with him. He knew I was doing it, too, because after a minute he looked down at me.

"Nothing?"

"What does HP stand for?" I blurted. It came out really loud. We'd already reached my driveway so I stopped walking and mumbled, "This is me."

"Old Man Sneider's place? You guys bought this house of horrors? Wow, when we were little, we used to hide behind this wall right here and watch for ghosts in the windows."

"Who did?"

"Me. Kids around here. This house was the only one that never got decorated on Halloween. It never needed to." HP sighed nostalgically. "And there used to be a shit-scary dog that lived here. I walked to school with a rock in my hand all of Grade Nine." He took his baseball cap off and ruffled the hair at the back of his neck. He had a line around his head from where he'd thrown his hat on after swimming. "You got a dog?"

"We had one back in Boston but it got re-gifted."

"By who?" He said it like he was about to get a posse together.

"Mom gave him to a family across town. I think it was a hair thing."

HP nodded like he understood the logic. We stared at each other. He stretched. "I'll walk by here tomorrow morning at eight. If you're here, you're here."

I pressed my back against the brick gatepost and looked up at him. "What's HP stand for?"

"My last name's Parker, but that's all you're getting." He put his baseball cap back on. "Some secrets you have to earn. I'll see you around, Little John."

He stalked off, his fifteen-year-old legs gangly in his skinny jeans. I watched him kick a pebble down the sidewalk, catching up, then punting it on. He did it all the way home.

From then on, the only days I didn't walk to school with HP were those when one of us was home sick. And as it turned out, the greatest alliance anybody in the school could have was with HP. I never had any trouble from anyone ever again, including Burbank and Moyzen.

As we got older—Grade 11—girls waited for him at the gates and he'd peel off, flapping me a wave as he joined hands with the latest one. He had a constant stream of female fans; I'd often be in the washroom

while a huddle of Grade 11s consoled the latest HP
casualty as she dabbed her eyes. *Shhh*, they'd whisper,
their eyebrows panicked. *That's her, that's Little John.
Wait till she leaves.*

Girls threw themselves at HP's feet, and he hadn't figured out who the good ones were yet. I doubt he even
cared. By seventeen he was captain of the swim team. He
had bright blue eyes and arms like Poseidon. Even Mr.
Cameron, the school principal, thought he was cool and
high-fived him in the lunchroom. HP called Mr. Cameron "Jerry" or, on some days, "Jer." When it came to the
girls, though, I wished HP would be pickier, and maybe
slow down a little on the hand-holding. Like my mom
always told me, it's graceless not to discriminate.

I never understood why HP had chosen me as his
friend, or how I'd gotten an all-access pass to him. It
was like having a key to the White House. He told me
everything he thought and felt and wanted, and I don't
think he told anyone else in the world—not even Ezra,
his best buddy. Ezra was a goofball and a jock, and if
you told him you even had a feeling about anything
he'd probably give you a charley horse and call you
a pansy. Sometimes HP painted pictures on thick, fibrous paper and wrote me letters over the top of them,
letters about the good things in life—how your skin
feels after a day in the ocean; the smell of asphalt before it rains; the way old people's hands wrap around

coffee cups in restaurants. Ezra would have punched HP in the face if he'd found out about those. I kept all of the letters—I still have them.

In the summer after Grade 11, HP and I sat with our backs against the trunk of the old birch tree in his front yard. We met there a lot, often after dinner when I'd walk the block barefoot and call for him at his open front door. His parents rarely shut the door and never locked it. "If anything's coming for us," HP's dad used to say, "it'll come just as good through a window."

It was a warm night—August, I think—and the cicadas were screeching. Mrs. Parker came out with pie, but I didn't want any.

"It's peach." HP took a plateful and a fork, hefting off a huge chunk.

"Are you sure, Angela?" HP's mom was small like a sparrow, with papery-soft skin. She spoke in short sentences and whenever she could, touched HP on the shoulder or head in passing.

"I'm fine, thanks, Mrs. Parker. I just ate."

"Don't get cold out here." She drifted back to the house. "You two. I don't know."

HP rolled his eyes. "She thinks we're soul mates. She said so at dinner. Says she's never seen two kids more comfortable." A couple of huge bites and the pie was gone. "I told her to stop being emotional."

"I like that." I picked up a leaf and ran its supple edge across my bare knee. "I believe in soul mates, but my mom says there's no such thing. She says there are tons of people a person could be with, not just one. Believing in a soul mate is like believing in Santa. According to her it's only ever about timing—who you meet and whether you're ready. That's all it is."

"Downer."

"Yeah." I moved my foot so it lined his. "That's what I said."

HP shuffled his back against the bark of the tree like a bear scratching. "Actually, you know what? I'm with your mom. There *are* tons of people a person can be with." He raised his eyebrows and brushed pie crumbs from his shirt.

"You're certainly testing the theory."

"So far not so many soul mates, though. More wing nuts than soul mates, if I'm keeping a tally."

I flung my leaf at his foot. "That's because you only date people on the outside."

"What does that mean?"

"You don't know who any of them are!"

He banged my knee with his knuckles. "How am I supposed to know they're wingers when I ask them out? It's like friending someone on Facebook and then realizing they're nuts when you look at their page. You've entered into a contract by then."

"Delete! Easy."

"Okay, well, we can be soul mates. I'll date the wingers and you can be my soul mate."

"Another healthy plan."

With my weight against his side I could feel the teenage-boy leanness of him through the fabric of his sweatshirt. I could have straightened back up but didn't.

"One more year of school." He sighed. I loved how his brain did that: the leaps were almost visible. "I can't wait to be done."

"Are you going to travel?"

We'd talked before about the adventures that were out there—the shark dives in South Africa, the climbing of the Matterhorn. But now our final year was before us, and with the freedom to pick a direction, the world seemed less conquerable. Going places was scarier than talking about them.

"I don't know. My dad's on me about getting a trade. He's offered me an apprenticeship with him as a carpenter." HP shrugged. "Sounds okay."

"God, what is it about parents who have only one child? My folks are on me constantly about which school this and what scholarship that. Jeez, it's like they had a kid just so they could obsess and over-steer and maybe get a second shot at the glory. You know what I'm talking about."

I felt HP wince and pull at the neck of his hoodie. "My folks aren't like that. They're just looking out for me. And the truth is I'm not an only child." He paused. "I had a brother."

The volume of the cicadas suddenly increased, or else it was the white noise in my head. I pushed myself up so I could look at him. "You what?"

"He died when I was four."

I thought of his quiet mother and his dad's apathy about locking the door. They already knew they couldn't keep the world out.

"Oh, HP, why didn't you tell me before? That's terrible."

"I don't talk about it a lot." He rubbed his eye. "And I don't want you to, either."

"No, of course—"

"I was only four. My brother choked at the dinner table right there." He nodded towards the kitchen window, which was open and amber with light. "I was sitting next to him. He was a year younger than me."

I must have made a sound then because he faltered and put his arm around me. I could feel his ribs against mine. "I don't remember a whole lot, just the fear of it. The panic. My dad wasn't home, just my mom."

"Christ."

HP breathed in and out once, lifting me and settling me back against the birch. "You know, life's not controllable. You do the best you can with the chances you get. And on you go."

"How didn't it kill your parents?"

"It did. It devastated them. But they went on. So did I, I guess."

He knew himself so well. He was miles ahead of me.

"Why didn't you guys move?"

"Because pain isn't in houses." He swallowed hard. "And when something like that happens, it ties you to the house. It's like a scar you grow into. I can't explain it." He picked up a twig and rolled the peeling bark with his thumb. "So I'll probably take the apprentice-ship with my dad, and the high school's making noise about me coaching their swim team. That sounds all right, too. I don't know about the travel thing."

"Jesus," I said, still reeling. "If I was you, I'd want a change of scene. Let's go somewhere else. We can go together."

"For what? To 'find ourselves'? Like I said, Little John, I'll be me wherever I go."

We sat silently for a few minutes, watching the light from inside HP's house. I could hear his mother clank-ing pots in the kitchen.

"I don't need to go anywhere, either," I said at last. "Here's fine for now."

He drew me into a hug and pulled his hood up, so

I could see only strands of beachy hair poking out and the strong line of his chin.

In the spring of Grade 12—so, eight years ago—my class planned a late-June camping trip out at Elbow Lake for grad. Mom was weird about me going, which was dumb, given how she'd dragged me all over the country growing up. Apparently her new thing was for me to stay home more.

"And will there be adult supervision?" She twisted the pearl earring in the lobe of her ear. She'd been chopping carrots and had flecks of peel stuck to the sinews of her forearm. Behind us on the counter her food-preparation *Les Misérables* blared: she'd turned it up just before I came in, and we had to shout over it to be heard. "And have you finished your paper on *Faust*? You need to maintain your grade point average, darling. Beat everyone else and finish strong."

"What?" I said, my head in the fridge. There was never anything good to eat: it was all baba ghanoush and tapenade. I pulled out a strawberry yogurt drink that HP must have left there.

"Honey, don't say *what*, say *pardon me*. And drinking yogurt is manly. Get a spoon." My mother's hair draped forwards over her shoulder as she worked, and she batted it away with a heavily bangled wrist.

"It's runny, Mom. The yogurt is *runny*!" I walked over and turned the CD volume down, then stood against the kitchen drawers, slurping from the container. My mother grimaced. "So can I go on the camping trip or what? Or *pardon me*?"

"Don't be clever, Angela. Nobody likes a show-off."

Dad wandered into the kitchen humming a Tchaikovsky bass line. It was rare to see him. When he wasn't working at the library, he spent every hour in his study at home poring over ancient Greece. He knew everything about Orpheus and nothing about me. When he reached for a slice of carrot, Mom slapped his hand.

"Who else is going?" She grasped the knife and chopped. This was the key answer to get right.

"HP." I waited.

Even the mention of his name swept light onto her face. Did women of all ages adore him? I rolled my eyes but she didn't catch me. Mom had decided long ago that I'd marry HP. I could ask her a question about anything else four times and she wouldn't hear me. Say HP's name, though, and her head snapped around like a barn owl's.

I'd been buddies with him for close to a year before I first introduced him to my mom. I wasn't much of a talker back then, and if my parents ever asked how school was going, I gave them only monosyllables. But one day Mom intercepted HP and me on our walk home.

"Oh, hi!" she said, not looking at me. "Who's your friend?"

HP readjusted the strap of his backpack and stood up straighter.

"I'm Shelley Petitjean"—Mom wheeled past me—"what a pleasure it is. Angela failed to mention she had such a handsome chaperone for the school commute."

"This is HP, Mom. He lives a block up."

"I bet he does."

HP gave my mom a kind of hybrid handshake–high five across the gate. "Pleased to meet you, Mrs. Petitjean."

"Oh, call me Shelley, for goodness' sake." Her finger pointed at his chest, making him glance down as if he'd spilled food there. "You're the quarterback on the football team." She tapped her lip. "No, wait, you're a junior hockey player. Beach volleyball?" She shook her head. "You've got me all turned around."

"He swims," I mumbled. "See you tomorrow, HP."

"HP? What does that stand for?"

He shifted his baseball cap.

"It's a secret," I said.

"Is it? Will you tell me later?" Mom whispered to me.

"So." HP cleared his throat. "Nice to meet you, Mrs. Petitjean. I'll see you around, LJ."

Mom looked at me quizzically, then looked back at HP. "Is there a prom soon? You should ask Angela to it."

"Mom!" I started to walk into the house. "It's, like, in a whole year's time and besides, gross."

Mom followed me in, waving good-bye as HP took off. "Angela, you need to plan ahead for your milestone moments." She hurried after me, stepping over my bag as I dropped it in the hall. "I'm telling you—Angela, stop moving and listen to me—prom's a major life event and that boy is your prom date. Milestone moments!"

Now at the kitchen counter, Mom paused in her carrot chopping. "Oh, darling, you didn't tell me *HP* was going camping. That's great. Now I know you'll be safe. He'll look after you."

"Well, hold on a minute, Shelley." Dad adjusted the waistband of his track pants over his dress shirt. He took his reading glasses off and held them up to the light, huffing hot breath onto each pane. "Is it an overnight thing?"

"Yes, Dad. It's a camping trip, with tents and sleeping."

"And we're sure that HP will keep a good eye on you, are we?"

"Of course we are, David. He adores her. Doesn't he, Angela?"

26

I shrugged.

"He adores her. You should see the way he looks at her." Mom sighed and put her hand to her bony chest, the edge of the knife blade glinting near her chin. "Although frankly, honey, you could make more of an effort. Is that a boy's sweater? And why do you insist on wearing your lovely dark bangs so they hang over your superior bone structure? If I were to take a photo of you right now and show it to you in ten years, you'd be horrified."

"You can only go if you've done all your homework," Dad said.

"I'll have graduated by then!"

"And if you have everything in place with college plans. Did I tell you I heard back from Reggie McIntosh? He's head of Classics at Oxford." He abandoned his search for crackers and rubbed his hands together while I yawned. "You might be in with a chance for this fall if you keep your head down. Reggie's working it so you take your freshman year over there—he owes me a favor, so he's all but sneaking you in the back door."

I drained the last of my yogurt.

"Oxford University, England—get excited, it doesn't get any more Ivy League than that! You have such potential, my dear . . ." He trailed off.

If he was waiting for thanks he didn't get it. I couldn't care less about Ivy League schools. The only

27

reason I went along with his push for academia was because it got me out of their crosshairs.

"We can talk about it properly another time . . . Angela? Look at me. Here's what I have to say about this camping trip: *If* all your work is done . . ." He raised a pale index finger. ". . . and you keep your wits about you, it should be acceptable. But be careful: I know how teenage boys think. I was one of them, too, you know."

"No, you weren't, David." Mom put her knife down and wiped her hands on her hips. She turned to me. "You can go, darling."

I turned *Les Misérables* back up. It had been easier than I'd thought.

So if all the other girls, including my mom, were crazy about HP, how did I feel about him? I know that's what you're thinking, Novak.

Was I in love with him? My mother would say I was, but she also drove us to prom with the theme tune from *Titanic* playing on her car stereo, so don't believe anything she says. Why was it so crucial that I define my feelings for him? If you ask me if he dominated my teenage years, that's an easier one to answer. The truth is I don't know if I was ever like the other girls. I knew HP too well. He was handsome; I liked seeing him with his shirt off; but when I caught myself looking at him, it felt kind of . . . obscene. We were friends. We were at ease and had no need to decipher ourselves. Not, at least, until after the camping trip.

chapter

3

We drove out to Elbow Lake in Ezra's beat-up old Chevy, Korn pumping from the stereo. Four of us had crammed into the front bench seat—Ezra driving; HP next to him; HP's current girlfriend, Lacy; and me.

Lacy's thigh pressed against mine, the sweat between us off-putting. Every now and then one of us would smear it off our legs while looking the other way. I didn't want to absorb anything she secreted. Her shoulders looked like moose antlers but, according to Ezra, she did a "mad nasty dance." Actually I wasn't sure what that was, but it sounded like a reason for an eighteen-year-old boy to date you.

For June, the sky blazed blue with the promise of

a great summer. Looking back, I see I was swept up with everyone's pure potential. We were done—free to go in whatever direction we chose, with a whole summer dedicated to nothing but one another. There was a camaraderie, a unity in our not-yet-knowing, and it was the first time I'd ever felt truly a part of something. Come fall, our grad class would hit the ground like marbles and scatter in fifty different directions, but for now we were free-falling. There are so few times like that in your life—when nothing is marked or limited by loss, when the possibilities seem endless and hopeful. I wanted to shout out loud at the world's infinity but with all the windows down in the truck, Lacy's long dark hair kept whipping into my mouth.

"You bring your bikini, Little John?" shouted Ezra, his dark eyebrows raised above the rim of his aviator sunglasses. "I'm hoping it has polka dots. You could totally pull that off."

HP shook his head and put his arm around Lacy, his hand grazing my shoulder, too. "She'll have brought her oversized men's T-shirt." He winked at me while I glared at him.

"Hidden treasures," said Ezra, nudging HP and passing him a beer. "I like a challenge."

They clinked beer cans. Even Lacy laughed.

"You're going to need a better map, boys." I pushed

past Lacy, squashing her back in her seat as I grabbed HP's beer from his hand. A crescent of amber lilted around the rim of the can, warmed by HP's mouth. As I sipped it, one elbow out of the window, I noted that Lacy wasn't smiling anymore.

We stopped at the liquor store on the outskirts of town. You'd think it would be hard for four under-age kids to get beer, but with HP it took about thirty seconds. When a fifty-year-old man in beige slacks walked out of the store carrying a bottle of vermouth, I swore and slouched farther down inside the truck, keeping one eye on HP.

"Shit, LJ, isn't that your old man?" Ezra hunched over the steering wheel.

"So busted," I breathed. Through the open window of the truck, we could hear that HP's whistling had stopped. The three of us gaped at him from twenty feet away—even Lacy, who had no knowledge of my dad.

"How are you, Mr. Petitjean?" HP's voice didn't waver.

My dad jumped and turned, hugging his blue glass bottle.

"Oh, HP. How're you doing? Are you loitering, dis-turbing the peace?" Dad laughed at his own question, his reedy shoulders raking up and down.

"I'm off to grad, sir. We're going camping."

"Oh, the camping trip. Yes, I heard about this one.

What a grand idea. Sleeping under Andromeda, the old twinkling face of Cassiopeia?"

HP can't have known what my dad was talking about, but his expression remained steady.

"Actually, young man, I was going to ask you, between us boys, to watch out for Angela. She's a bright girl with an exciting future. I'm sure you've noticed."

HP nodded.

"And do you know of her plans for college?"

He didn't because I had none.

Dad's narrow head tilted. "Did you want to ask me?"

"Not about that, sir, no. But could you maybe help a guy out?"

No way. No way was HP going to ask my dad to buy us beer.

"It's grad, after all . . ." I heard HP say before my dad blocked our view of him and everything became muffled.

I watched my dad scratch the top of his messy hair, take hold of HP by one shoulder and lean in close. Then he walked back into the store. HP put both arms straight up into the air and grinned at us, lowering them quickly again as my dad reemerged and handed HP a case of Budweiser. "One each, remember, and none for my daughter." He strolled towards his car with his vermouth.

"Legend!" shouted Ezra when HP got back in the truck. "That's your best one yet!"

HP scrambled past my knees and wedged himself back in next to his girlfriend. He yanked at his buckle, whooping. "I don't know why you complain about your folks so much, Little John. Your dad's awesome."

"What did you say to him at the end?"

"I just told him the truth. What? You never thought of that before?"

"Why is it always so easy . . . ?" I began, but Ezra bounced us off the curb of the parking lot and onto the highway, and I never finished the thought.

"What if we get pulled over?" Lacy asked as we raced away.

"We won't." HP cranked the stereo and shifted to look at me. "All good, John? Are you mad I asked your dad?"

I shrugged. "My parents understand you better than they do me. Or just plain like you better."

"What's not to like?" he yelled as he passed me a can and slapped me on the collarbone. "And it's not a competition. Drink this and stop thinking."

"Big Bad Grad!" Ezra shouted, honking his horn. We roared along the highway away from town. I sipped a Budweiser and wondered how I would ever in my life be able to leave this place without HP, since the world rolled open only for him.

33

For a small town with a graduating class of less than fifty, the crowd at Elbow Lake was already edging a hundred. Two docks led out from the shore, rickety and rusty-nailed. To the left of the beach, a forest began, and grads of years gone by had built a bunch of tree platforms in there with rope ladders up to them. Hundreds of lanterns hung from branches— unlit, spiderwebbed and rusting—and the forest bark was scarred with an alphabet of former alumni. We drove towards the scattering of tents, veering off the track and over the grass, our shoulders bumping as we hit potholes in the turf.

"What are we sleeping in?" Lacy glanced from face to face.

"We'll sleep when we're dead, Lace," said Ezra, and he threw the truck into park. He shut off the engine, clambering out onto the hood. "The party's arrived!" He reveled in the sunlight, his black hair cut short at the sides in a fauxhawk, his teeth white against his tanned face. The swim team whooped in response, swelling towards him like a tide.

"Have you brought a tent?" Lacy tucked hair behind her ear and pressed her knees together.

"Too late now," said HP. "We'll be fine. I have my man blanket."

"It's plaid," I told her.

I pushed open my door and got out of the truck.

Ezra swooped down and grabbed my arm, hauling me upwards towards him. He waltzed me around on the hood of his truck in a high-kneed cowboy swirl, the curve of his bicep pressing tight against my shoulder. He smelled of laundry soap. On the second spin I saw Lacy and HP turn their faces up at us—her brow milk-pale, his darkening.

I sat on the dock for a lot of the afternoon, dangling my toes in the water. Bugs skittered on the surface, spindly with heat. Classmates thundered behind me along the dock to launch into the cool of the lake, and from time to time HP came and sat next to me to skim stones.

"I'd push you in," he said, "but I think you'd drown under the weight of your T-shirt. Why no bathing suit?"

"I'm not like Lacy."

"Do you shower with your eyes closed?" He stood and turned, balancing on his toes on the dock edge. His stomach muscles were tight, and his arms wound windmills to balance. "You're way prettier than you think, Little John. You have this whole funky-ass style thing going on and you don't even know it. Why else would Ez be moving in on you?" I must have bunched up my eyebrows at him because he added, "Christ, you walk around with your eyes closed, too." He teetered then backflipped into the lake.

By five everyone was hungry and HP built a fire and got out wieners, the only food anyone had thought to bring besides potato chips. The sun had freckled HP's shoulders, and the edges of his hairline looked dusted with sand. Lacy draped around him as he tried to blow life into the fire; her makeup was impeccable and she'd piled her hair high on top of her head to avoid getting it wet in the lake. My mother would have applauded her.

A girl to my left nudged me and passed me a joint, the end of which had been sucked closed into a mulch of ten people's saliva. I shook my head and she shrugged—a *suit yourself* shrug—like I thought I was better than her or something. HP caught it.

"Hey, Julia, why don't we dip this hot dog bun in the lake and pass it around?" he said.

A bunch of people laughed and I caught HP's eye across the fire. He was protecting me. I'd only smoked pot once and that was with him, in his room with the window open, and I didn't leave his house for four hours in case his parents asked me a question on the walk through the living room. Julia threw the droopy joint into the fire. Some guy named Billy had brought a guitar with him, and as the sun began to slide behind the trees he strummed Pink Floyd tunes and all the girls swayed back and forth together like wheat.

"Jesus fuck." Ezra strode out from the woods. "What is this, Brownie camp?"

He turned the key in his truck's ignition and Korn fired up again. Billy put his guitar away as Ezra started a game of Truth or Dare, and soon everyone was shouting against the music, girls coyly avoiding questions and slinking into boys' laps to lock lips with them.

I walked away then. I hadn't kissed a boy yet. Don't get me wrong, I wasn't scared and I'd definitely thought about it: I wondered what it would be like to breathe in someone else's breath and have someone's eyes really look into mine. As a child, my mother read me nothing but Prince Charming stories at bedtime, and as much as I scorn that now, I have to agree you shouldn't waste kisses on the wrong boys. I wasn't like most teenagers: I gave value to true intimacy. I wanted a kiss to mean something.

Ezra must have gotten the party zone ready because every tree twinkled with lantern lights and all the rope ladders hung low. I tiptoed along the path, pausing to feel the bark of the oldest trees. I've always loved forests—the way the light filters, the stillness, what the trees witness and never tell. I heard a heavy footfall behind me and turned to see Ezra striding along the pine trail, his sleeveless plaid shirt flapping over a bare chest.

"There you are," he said.

The dimple in the tanned cheek was working over-time. He hooked both hands onto a high rung of a rope ladder. I stood uncomfortably against a tree.

"Want to climb up there with me?" He nodded at the platform above our heads.

"Not really." What was he up to?

"Want to dance?" He let the rope ladder swing him towards me.

"There's no music." I couldn't decide if my heart was beating so fast because he scared or interested me. His chest was lined with muscle.

"Lighten up, LJ." He unhooked his hands from the ladder and placed them on each side of my head. "Who needs music?"

The sweetness on his breath was more pungent than beer. He stared directly at my mouth, hesitated and shuffled his feet in closer. His arms bent so his whole upper torso pressed against me. He leaned into my lips.

"Wait."

"Wait?"

The thing I have to admit is, Ezra was hot: he was all Italian-heritage genes and chocolate eyes and his mouth looked like he'd just been eating strawberries. Girls went nuts over Ezra—he was the other one they cried about in the washrooms.

"Let's do this"—he kissed the side of my jaw—"and

see what happens." As he brought his mouth towards mine, I must have cringed because he stopped. "Or not." He pushed off the tree and stretched his arms out above his head, yawning his rejection away. "Wow. Shut down. I didn't see that coming."

"I'm just not—"

"It's all good, Little John. Whatever. I just wanted to try something out."

I took the bait. "Try what out?"

"I just think it's time you put your cards on the table."

"What table?"

"Come on, LJ. You're smokin' hot but nobody can lay a finger on you and us guys, we're all wondering why that is. You're like a virgin island and I got to tell you—we're ready to travel."

I grimaced. "Who's 'us guys'?"

"You know . . . *the* guys. Kaden, Jared, Calen, Caleb, Jayden . . ." He listed weirdly identical names from the water polo team, counting them off on his fingers.

"Maybe I have taste. Or standards. Or . . . or taste."

Ezra crouched until he was sitting on the pine-needled path.

"And more than two brain cells to rub together." I kicked my heel back against the tree trunk.

"Easy, easy. Don't blow up that big college brain of yours. Come, check this view out."

39

He patted the ground beside him. Another pat and I relented and sat down. Ezra was likable, even when he was being a jerk. We lay side by side on the ground like kids in the snow, looking up at the patchwork sky.

"So you're saying," he persisted, "you're picky because you have standards. But I wonder. Is. That. Really. It." He stroked his chin, faux-meditatively. "Or is it more that you're waiting for someone to look at you a certain way?"

"Who?" It was almost a shout. I could feel my face reddening.

"Who?" he repeated.

"You two sound like owls, who-who-ing," said a deep voice. Ezra and I strained our necks to see HP standing by our feet.

"Where'd you come from?" My voice sounded squeaky.

"The fire."

"We're making pine angels," I mumbled.

"I see that."

"I tried to make out with your buddy here, but she shut me down. Rude." Ezra scrambled to his feet, dusting needles from the back of his pants. "I was just getting to the bottom of why she'd do that, since if I wasn't me, I'd hit on me. Right?"

"You're asking would I hit on you?" HP picked up

a pinecone, considered it for a moment, then whipped it into the trees.

Ezra paused. When he spoke again he sounded cautious. "Where's your girlfriend?"

"Skinny-dipping, I think. A dare."

"Dude! Here, take this." Ezra tossed a rolled-up plastic bag from his pocket at HP. "I'll see you guys back at the fire. Or tomorrow, on the other side. Whichever comes first." He hurried off down the path towards the fire pit and the lake, leaving HP and me alone.

"Skinny-dipping, huh?"

"Yep."

We sat knee against knee, the tree behind our backs. HP was wearing his signature pale-blue hoodie, the crest of his blond hair fluffy from an afternoon swimming in the lake water. The light in the woods was dusky, not dark, and shadows skittered on the forest floor.

"Didn't want to join her, huh?"

"Didn't want to make out with him, huh?" HP banged his knees together, bumping mine.

"I'm picky."

"I told you he was into you."

"He's not into me. He's drunk and eighteen."

"Shit, Little John. Take a compliment for once." He unrolled the plastic bag Ezra had given him and sniffed inside it. "Oh, no. That's not good."

41

I took the bag and held it up in the shadows. "What is that? It smells like . . . mold."

"Magic mushrooms. Want to try some?"

HP wasn't a drug kind of guy—that one time we got high was an anomaly. HP was too athletic, too competitive, too 10k-run-before-school. He took out a dried, papery mushroom and bit the end of it, chewing like a camel.

"Not so bad. Here, try one. What's the worst that can happen?"

We stared at each other as we chewed.

"They taste like the stuff they put on your tongue in church," I said.

"They taste like dusty cow patties."

"How many of those have you eaten before?"

"How often do you go to church?"

We sniggered and HP took my hand.

"Let's hold tight," he said, and in that moment we left everyone at the party behind and it became him and me and the night ahead.

'm sorry to go on about recreational drugs in a police station, Detective Novak; I know that's inappropriate. But this is about me and HP. This is *our* story, even if it has taken enough twists that I'm telling it in here. There's a unique closeness that comes from two friends doing drugs like that together, and I don't care if that's illegal. HP and I were already close—always had been—but with our minds adjusted we clung to each other as if we were visitors on this planet and mutually surprised by it.

Ezra had said once that taking mushrooms was like dipping the sponge of your brain into more water, a metaphor I thought was dumb until I knew what he meant. Every day the world dances around you, a semaphore sending signals, offering beauty, waiting to be noticed, but your undistorted brain can't process the gifts and sends them back unopened. There's a whole other dimension on offer every minute, and on drugs your head tilts and shows you what's out there. I haven't done mushrooms since then and probably won't ever again; I had my night. What's the point of doing something twice when it's been done perfectly the first time? It's the same reason I won't fall in love now.

We spent a lot of that night up on a tree platform, looking down as people milled on the path below us while music pumped from speakers with a bass beat that pulsed inside my skin. HP's face seemed mottled in blue-green algae, and I was sure the platform was a raft, adrift on a gentle sea. Time blurred unhelpfully and neither of us had a watch. As night pushed further towards morning, the lantern lights in all the trees fizzed and faded like a colony of eyes shutting.

I turned to HP. "I think I can climb down the rope

now." I tucked my hair behind my ears and felt it tickle my earlobes.

"Let's try. Wow, your eyes are amazing. They're slate gray. And it's, like, morning and I'm not even hungry. What's up with that?"

HP reached forwards and grabbed the top of the rope ladder. Gingerly he stretched down, ramming his sneaker onto a foothold. Then he waited for me, guiding my skate shoe until it felt safe. The pine needles were spongy under our feet as we walked out of the woods past clusters of grads smoking joints, their legs plaited together, girls' heads on boys' shoulders.

The fire pit smoked alone, beer cans littering the circle. We walked beyond it holding hands. At the top of the smooth curve of hill was a patch of grass where we threw ourselves onto our knees.

"Tell me something real," I said.

HP rubbed his jaw, which glinted golden with stubble. "Want to know my first name?" He paused. "H is for Hamish. My grandfather's a Scot."

"Hamish Parker." I grinned. "I can't believe it took you so long to tell me."

"Well, you earned it." He turned his head, squinting. "Although you could have asked the school secretary. I'm pretty sure it's in all the records."

We laughed. After a pause I spoke again.

"What was your brother's name?"

HP closed his eyes. "Thomson. He was blonder than me and funner."

It was all he'd say.

We lay still on the steepness of the slope, a couple in a luge event, rigid and straight-armed, hurtling somewhere unknown. He fell asleep almost immediately, snoring quietly with his hands resting on his chest. His long eyelashes fluttered with dreams. Awake alone, I glanced up at the scuffed sky. It's always been companionable to me—I like its unending stretch, and the notion that wherever you go it's with you. My brain flexed and in a melt of cheekbones and lips, the clouds morphed into a kind, wizened old man with a face that was benevolent and warm. After that every cloud that rolled by became an exercise in changing clouds into figures—monks, wizards . . . and monsters. I learned, right there in the grass, that what you see each day is entirely your own invention. I found out that night that I could alter what's in front of me—I could literally write the sky.

When I woke it was warm sunshine. HP was sitting up, bare-chested with his hoodie knotted around his waist. His back muscles tightened and relaxed as he plucked at strands of grass.

"Hey," I croaked. He turned, the side of his mouth breaking into a grin.

"How d'you feel? A little less than average?" He lay down on his side, his head resting on his hand while he sucked a piece of grass. His pectoral muscle was heavy and grooved.

"I'm too hot." I lurched and sat up to pull off my white T-shirt. Underneath I wore a small tank top. The morning air felt good on my shoulders. "Where is everyone?" I turned to catch HP staring at me.

He cleared his throat and pointed back down towards the fire pit, where people were starting to wander around. Someone had started a fresh fire, and we could hear it snapping as the flames licked.

"Here, I got you this."

He passed me a bottle of cold water. I cracked the cap, drinking in the clean coolness like a shipwreck survivor.

"Where did you find these?"

"By Ez's truck. He left a cooler there all night. I've been up for about an hour."

He ran his grass strand down the skin of my shoulder and I wriggled, batting at him with a limp palm.

"Guess where my girlfriend slept last night. I'll give you three guesses and the first two don't count." He flung the grass strand into the field while I looked at him carefully.

"Does it matter?"

He let out one bark of a laugh. "No; but I might kick the shit out of Ezra on principle."

I used my hand like a visor and peered down the hill.

There was Lacy on Ezra's lap, wearing his grad jacket. Her hair looked like she'd run it through a hedge.

"Maybe he just wants the things you have. Or maybe she does."

His brow had a tiny V in the center, his trademark stamp of deep thought. "At least you had the sense to not make out with him."

"I told you. There's no point kissing the wrong boy."

I'm certain there was a beat where we stared at each other, where we wondered if we were thinking the same thing. A second. A half second. Was it his hand or mine that moved first? All I remember clearly is that the world suddenly felt fluid. In one flow of motion, his hand was behind my neck and I rolled onto the skin of his chest. Our heat-seeking mouths felt warm on the inside, our tongues sliding and smooth. My whole body pulsed in ways I hadn't known before. The more I kissed him, the more I wanted. I tasted his neck; inhaled the smell of him, his beach-smoked oak. The buttons of our jeans snagged as we pressed together.

"We have to go somewhere," he gasped.

I was struck dumb by an ache to have his mouth back.

"Ezra's truck," I suggested. It stood parked just twenty feet away with the tailgate open, the nose facing down the hill so the back end was entirely hidden. We ran there, half crouching as if under fire. HP hauled me up into the truck bed and unrolled his man blanket for us to lie on. He climbed on top of me, although he held back some of his weight because I could feel his triceps muscles tense when my fingers brushed them. We slowed down.

"Do you feel weird?" he asked, so close that I felt the words on my face.

"No. Do I?"

He shook his head, earnest, the fluff at his crown sticking up. I arched up for him, pulling him onto me. As the world blurred around us, dream-like, I couldn't believe we were really doing this. Confidence beat from me: I know it was me who undid the first pant fly, who slid fingers under his waistband. My hands moved on him as if they'd already lived this scene, already knew what happened next.

He moaned and twisted, whispered, "Are you sure you haven't been practicing?"

And we smile-kissed, free with the sky looking down on us, surprised by the rightness we'd discovered.

That early morning with HP was an *on* switch I never thought we'd flick. Once we'd found it, the light fell differently on us. I'd never been naked before—not like that. Suffice to say I didn't know I had those instincts until I found them with him.

chapter

4

As I speak, all these memories flood me and I'm back in the past, alive there, with all the light the same. I go quiet for long stretches, following pathways of old thoughts right to their very end, enjoying the camber of voices I recognize. So many perfect days are stored in my head. Novak brings me back if I take too long, and I try to let him see the moment I've just relived. I'm not sure if I can, though—not to any real depth. It's one of life's great sadnesses, surely, the inability to properly convey. But I'm trying.

woke up in Ezra's truck, pulling the fleece of the blanket around my ribs as I peeped over the rim of the truck bed. There were my classmates packing up camp, stamping out the fire, gathering up chip packets—I don't know how long we'd slept but the sun was high in the sky and Ezra was starting the climb up the hill towards us.

"HP!" I shook his shoulder, rocking him out of the depths of sleep. "We have to get dressed!" I reached for my clothes, scrunched in a pile beside him.

"Hi." He pulled me against him and nuzzled into my neck.

"They're walking right up the hill."

He stretched and yawned, his mouth cavernous.

"Get clothes on!" I squeaked, trying to bat his hands away as I fastened my bra.

"You look good when you're freaking out. Your eyes get even bigger." He pulled on his pants and sat up. "Listen. Slow down a second. I just want to say something." I let him pull me over towards him and when he kissed me we were hungry again in a surge, our hands on each other's faces.

It was Ezra who separated us. He clanked the cooler HP had pilfered into the truck and hopped up on the tailgate, his back to us.

"Well, well, well." Ezra lit a cigarette and turned to face us. "Look who's graduated." He picked up my tank top and twirled it on his forefinger. I grabbed it. "You better get shoes on, bro. Your girlfriend's ten steps away."

HP said nothing but leapt over the side of the truck and sauntered down to the lake as Lacy arrived at the tailgate in Ezra's grad jacket.

"Where did he go?" she asked, watching me roll up his man blanket.

"HP, HP, HP." Ezra blew smoke rings and pinched a strand of tobacco from between his front teeth as Lacy took off down the hill again. "We all need HP."

He looked startled when I grabbed his cigarette and took a drag. "Since when do you smoke?"

"You don't know me like you think you do, Ez." I inhaled deeply, coughing while trying to seem like I'd done it before. "And FYI, HP's gonna kick your ass."

"Oh, get real. As if he's into Lacy." He grabbed the cigarette back. "Lacy's gonna kick *your* ass."

We glanced down the hill to see that Lacy had caught up to HP by the fire pit. He put his hands on his hips as he stood listening to her. She tried to touch his bare shoulder but of course he stepped back. I watched as he zipped up Ezra's grad jacket for her before walking back towards us.

"It's like a line dance where the partners switch," Ezra said. "We've all gone do-si-do."

We drove back to town, our formation along the front seat the same: I was still jammed up against Lacy and could feel the hate burning out of her towards the side of my head. I didn't look at her. The boys must have sorted out their differences with a few loose sentences while they packed up the truck; they both shouted song lyrics as we drove through town.

When Ezra parked outside my house, I got out to grab my bag from the back. Through the study window, I could see Dad slowly pacing the room as he read a piece of paper in his hands.

"See you guys soon," I said. "Thanks for the ride, Ez."

"Later." HP winked at me.

As I walked up the steps of the front porch, Dad emerged with a letter, which he waved so eagerly his hair bobbed. I walked right past him and into the house. Mom was doing sudoku on the couch, rubbing out a number she'd gotten wrong. As I walked into the living room, she looked up with the eyes of someone expecting a wedding announcement.

"So? How did it go? Sweetheart, tell me everything."

She patted the cushion next to hers, but instead I dropped my bag on the floor and trudged straight to the fridge.

"Was it wonderful? Did HP look after you?"

I drank milk straight from the carton but she was too enraptured to notice.

"I remember my grad weekend. I danced all night with Kenny Calahan and darling, I can tell you, he was no slouch. He drove me home in his father's BMW. It purred like a cat. I love a man in a Beamer."

"Is that why you chose Dad?" I snorted, looking around to see where he'd gone. He must have retreated back to his study.

"I didn't meet Dad until I was twenty-two! We were in *Twelfth Night* together; he was Malvolio, which was unattractive, but he charmed me at the cast party. I've told you this story before."

"I wasn't listening."

She shut her sudoku book and used it to fan her regal face. "These number puzzles are meant to be the easy level. The hard ones must be an entrance exam for NASA." Her laugh was too shrill. She got up and joined me in the kitchen, leaning in her swirly chiffon blouse against the countertop. "Angela, did you kiss a boy?"

I jumped at the question. "Why do you ask that?"

"Oh, I know a thing or two about my daughter." She twirled the yellow tie of her blouse between long, painted fingernails. "Look at your glow! You did kiss a boy, although why one would choose you with your hair a mess is beyond me. Was it HP? Oh, Angela, you have no idea how good you've got it." She sighed moonily. "There's nothing better than fresh love, and that boy's a diamond in a town of rough. Please tell me it was HP."

I put the milk back in the fridge and closed the door. "I've been thinking. I don't want to go away to college. I don't want to go anywhere."

"Don't be so ridiculous." Her voice dropped low and husky.

"It's what Dad wants. Nobody's asked me." I smeared milk off my top lip with the back of my hand while she took a deep breath.

"Did you take chemical drugs? You look peaked. You'll feel differently when you've had a hot shower and some fresh fruit. Your father has very exciting news for you. Where is he? He's been pacing the study all morning like a Bengal tiger. It's a relief you're home."

"Jesus, Mom. Can you not hear anything I'm saying?"

She swept back to the couch and arranged her skirt around her knees. "Let's not talk about it now, sweetheart. Not when your tone is this acidic."

"Let's not talk about what?" asked Dad as he shuffled into the living room. He stood behind the couch with his hands on his hips and his pelvis arched forwards. The letter he'd waved at me at the front door was now rolled up like a scroll, pressed tight against his hip bone.

"David, where have you been?"

"I had to go and fetch the envelope. Look at it! It's gold-crested." He rocked up to his tiptoes and back down again.

"I think now's not the time. No, David, she's addled and needs sleep. Look at her skin tone. I say we wait

54

on the good news." Mom leafed through the pages of her book.

"Oh," said Dad. He scratched the back of his neck. "What did you learn at grad camp? I hope HP didn't let me down."

"They've had an adventure," smiled Mom, nibbling the end of her sudoku pencil, "but she's being coy and well-mannered about it. A lady never kisses and tells."

Dad frowned. "Angela, we need to have a team talk about your future." He raised the rolled scroll of letter as if it were a trumpet through which he might bugle-horn his triumph. "I have Oxford developments to report." He took a step closer to the breakfast bar. "Angela, close the fridge and look at me. My darling, I know you're tired but we've gotten you into Oxford University, England! It's really happening! You're going to the best school in the *world*." He covered his lips with the fingertips of one hand and waited for me to celebrate.

"I'm not going anywhere."

His hesitation was momentary, like perhaps he hadn't been speaking English properly. "Reggie McIntosh has secured a freshman year of study for you to read Classics, based on what he's calling a 'superior academic transcript.' You'll be attached to Hertford College—they've also accepted you. Well done!"

I grimaced. Why hadn't I written worse papers through Grade 12?

"Angela, it's the kind of launchpad we could only have dreamed of. The possibilities coming out of this are endl—"

"I didn't dream of it. It's not my dream." In my head all I could see was HP, his face above mine in Ezra's truck.

Over on the sofa, my mother clamped her hands between her knees. "Oh, come on, darling, try and be positive. This is the ultimate milestone! We're handing you the keys to the kingdom."

"Nobody's asked me what I want!"

"I thought you'd be over the moon." My dad gaped at me like I'd told him learning was wrong.

"HP will wait for you, you know." Mom got up suddenly from the couch, and her puzzle book clattered to the floor.

"This is about HP?" asked Dad.

I said nothing.

"It's eight months abroad, Angela. Eight months that will set you up for the rest of your life. After that, you can have it *all*." Her eyes shone.

"I don't want it all."

"You're beautiful and gifted, darling." She swept hair from her brow. "You'll be opening doorways you can walk through with whoever you want. HP, for instance, would be a lovely choice. Nobody's disputing that. But Oxford? You absolutely must go."

"There's no backing out now," my dad said, wringing the back of his neck with one hand. "I've called in a favor and done all this groundwork. It'll be very humiliating." His toes pigeoned in worn-out slippers.

I was beginning to stand up to my mom, but my father was harder to defy. His good intentions held all of his own life's ruin. Arguing with him was like picking a fight with a limping dog.

Right then our phone rang and I swiped it from the wall, plugging my other ear and hunching over.

"Gray eyes?" It was HP's voice, deep and rich. I turned so that Mom couldn't see me. "Meet me in ten minutes outside your house."

"But I can't; I haven't even—"

"Do it later. We'll sleep when we're dead!"

I hurried out, as Dad's and Mom's eyes tracked me in disbelief.

When I think about that morning now, Detective Novak, I wish I'd said more, done more to defend my own future. Because if you don't protect that, who's going to do it for you? Oxford University, England, was never my pick; and yet it forged pathways going forwards that crept and thickened like vines. I'm not saying I know what's happened to Saskia, Detective, but I do know this: she only exists at all because of me.

chapter

5

Novak's let me talk with hardly an interruption, allowing me my forum, my monologue. I didn't expect him to stick to that deal. From time to time he'd glanced up when I paused, but as soon as I spoke again his focus had returned to the page, where he'd carried on scribbling with his dented pen. Now, though, he stops me. He's making a bid for the reins.

"So there's no doubt, then. It is a love story." Novak sticks his middle finger into his ear and twists it like he might dislodge something serious. Perhaps it explains his inability to listen properly.

I grab the bottle of water he brought me and crack the lid, drinking thirstily. "Like I said, Detective

Novak, what love story ends in a police station interview room?"

"You'd be surprised." He buttons his suit jacket. "What about *Romeo and Juliet*? I heard that doesn't end well."

"Not for the lovers."

"Are you saying Saskia's dead?" he asks.

We lock eyes. Everything's a game with this guy. The words aren't out of my mouth before he's jumping on them, turning them into something that suits his little checklist. I'm telling him what happened—as much as I know of it. But guys like him want a story they've heard before and they only ask questions if they already know the answers.

"What makes you think Saskia's Juliet?" I ask.

He clicks the end of his ballpoint pen in and out, in and out.

"What about *Jane Eyre*? Do you like that novel, Angela?"

My stomach tightens. He's been in my room; he's seen my bedside table. How else could he know to ask about that book? Novak's a guy who is good at watching and copying. But you know what? I'm good at watching, too. I can spot a fake. He hasn't read the classics, and for all Novak's studied meticulousness, there's toothpaste on his tie, smudged, like he rubbed at it with his thumb on the drive to work.

He steeples his fingers like a church spire. "Angela, are you the crazy one? Have you been locked away in the attic all these years?"

"In *Jane Eyre* it's the wife who's crazy and burns the whole house down, Detective. I've never been anybody's wife."

He scribbles notes while I sit with my arms crossed.

"Carry on." He reels his forefinger at me as if winding invisible thread and then reaches down into a briefcase he's had at his feet all morning. It's almost two o'clock. He pulls out a pear and something wrapped in waxed paper and places them gently on the table in front of me. Within the folds of the paper is a sandwich with the crusts cut off. Some kind of fish paste lingers in the stagnant air. He slices up the pear with a pocket-knife and offers a sliver to me.

"No appetite?"

"You'd better write that down in my file."

"You seem a little agitated. Would you like to tell me why that is?"

"I don't know why I'm here!" I hadn't meant to shout it. I take a deep breath. "I've done nothing wrong. I mean—am I in trouble or am I just helping you? Jesus, have you seriously searched my house?"

He rubs his hands together like he's watching television and this is his favorite bit.

"We brought you in under PC—probable cause. At

this point, we're just talking and you're not the only one we've brought in. You're not charged with anything."

"So I can leave?"

He takes a silver pocket watch out of the breast pocket of his suit. How pretentious. He flips the silver lid open, then snaps it closed again. "Let's say you can leave in roughly eighteen hours."

I cover my face with my hands.

"Keep going with your . . . story."

"What is it you want to know?"

He sighs. "Let's talk a little more about Saskia. You know her quite well, don't you? Despite the fact that you're talking about everyone *except* her?"

I look up at him, my face hard.

"I mean, it says here you shared a residence in Cove with both her and HP recently, and for several weeks. Can you confirm that? Your name isn't on the title of the house. His is."

"Yes. I shared a house with HP."

"I'm sure there's an interesting story behind that. You graduated eight years ago, so you're twenty-six—am I getting that right? And you do have your own address in town?"

I nod. "My parents owned a small house—I mean, an extra one. They had two places. I was living in the smaller one for the past six years or so, but my parents got divorced recently, so my mother moved in with me."

"Does your father still live in Cove?"

"Nope. After the divorce, my dad sold our old family home and took off for the coast to get away from my mother's endless judgment. I don't really know how he's doing. He calls now and then to check I'm okay."

"Are you?"

"More okay than he is."

Novak licks his thumb and forefinger. "So while your mother moves into the smaller house, you move into Mr. Parker's?"

"HP offered me his spare room so I could have some space until my mom felt better. She can be high-maintenance. Have you met her yet?"

"So yesterday, when Saskia disappeared . . ." He looks up. "Where were you?"

"Like I already told the other cops, I was home last night. With my mom. Detective Novak, I really don't think Saskia's even missing. She's probably staged this whole thing to get attention."

"What is it about Saskia that makes you feel competitive?" One of his eyebrows sits higher than the other.

I stop myself, breathe. "She's a fake. She lies about everything. I knew it the minute I met her."

He stretches luxuriously. "I see. So tell me a little bit more about all that."

My shoulders slump forwards and I cover my face with my hands again. It's impossible to finish a conversation with this guy. After a few seconds I look up. "Is HP here? Do you have him in one of these rooms?"

"We're speaking with several people. And we think you're protecting somebody. If you're not telling us everything, you put yourself in a dangerous position. Have you considered that?"

I reach over and grab a slice of his pear, shoving it into my mouth sideways and speaking while I chew. "You know what I think has happened? Saskia's probably lying low, licking her wounds."

His eyes narrow. "What wounds? Is she unhappy? Is that what you're saying?"

"Define *happiness*." I grab another glossy crescent of pear and drop it into my mouth.

Novak sits back. "I'd rather *you* defined her unhappiness for me. Why might she have felt wounded, Angela?" He crosses his arms, marking the end of his input. For now, it's back to me.

chapter
6

What Detective Novak will never understand is that I know what real happiness looks like. I lived it with HP that summer and the memories are burned in my mind.

We'd spend entire days together at the lake—him on the Tarzan swing while I read a novel in oversized sunglasses. He'd drop me home for dinner, much to my mom's delight, and then show up again in an hour and we'd go for a drive in his truck to the lake, or head up to the old mill site to make out. Every time a new movie came to town we sat together near the front, like couples did, while Ezra threw popcorn at us from the back row. We slept all night in his truck a bunch of times, even when I had curfew. We'd wake early, our noses cool, and burrow down under his man blanket until the sun seared us out into the day. We were inseparable.

Each weekend, there were pit parties out on Old Creek Road where our classmates drank from kegs, hanging out on truck tailgates. I'd turn up late and strain to find HP in the crowd, but when I saw him my body relaxed. I can't stand parties: I don't like the chaos. Lacy turned up to every one of those gatherings, too, desperately pivoting a toe in the dirt on the periphery of all conversation, just biding her time until HP had drunk enough beers that she could squirm into his ear with various propositions.

"She's a goddamn train wreck," Ezra said as we sat on a rock at the end of summer, watching HP unwrap Lacy from his waist for the tenth time. "It's so hot."

"You're disgusting," I murmured, but I took the cigarette he passed me.

Ezra put his arm around my neck. "You have so much to learn about guys."

"Don't kid yourself, Ez, it's a one-page manual."

I was bluffing. My summer with HP was filled with new discoveries. Every day I got closer to him, swam deeper, so much so that by the end of August I felt like I was breathing at the bottom of a warm ocean, looking up at the surface where all I used to do was paddle. I didn't want it to end, but like a hangnail snagging at the very back of my mind were my college plans for fall. I hadn't been able to turn Oxford down—I couldn't do it to my father. And as Mom kept pointing out, the family reputation was at stake. Besides, she was right about one thing: I wanted to get out of my parents' house and our rinky-dink town, even if I still couldn't imagine leaving without HP. How would I manage without him for eight months? At night in my own bed, I lay awake blinking at shadows. I hadn't found a way to tell him.

HP joined us on the rock, shaking his head as he sat down. "Lacy's the Terminator."

"I dig that level of desperation in a girl." Ezra nodded. "I was just teaching LJ what guys want."

To the left of us on the dirt road someone poured kerosene onto a pile of twigs and threw in a lit match. The bonfire thumped into flame to a chorus of cheers.

"I think she knows what we want." HP pulled me towards him.

"You two should just get married and get it over with." Ezra stubbed out his cigarette near my thigh. "Do us all a favor."

"I'm totally in if you are." HP grinned at me, kissing the side of my neck. I nodded but my shoulders were tight, and HP sensed it. "What's up with you, John?"

"These parties are all the same. The music's the

same, the drinks are the same and nobody has anything interesting to talk about." I scratched at a bump
of moss on the rock. "Summer's curling at the edges.
Everyone should just get the hell out of here."

Both boys looked sideways at each other.

"Okay . . . I'm down with leaving. Say the word."
HP stood up and dusted off his jeans. "Or . . . is that
not what you mean? What's the deal with you tonight?
You're . . . spiky."

"I'm bored."

Ezra took a lazy drag of a fresh cigarette. "Bullshit.
You're mad about something. I know girls."

"Let's get out of here," HP said quietly. "Unless it's
me you're mad at."

"It's not." I rolled the dead moss off the rock and
looked up. "Can you drive me home?"

We parked in my parents' driveway. As HP switched
off the stereo, he asked, "Is it something I did?"

I stared at my hands. "HP, I don't know what to say."

There was a tapping at my passenger window and
I glanced up to see my mother standing beside my
door in her dress coat. She'd recently brushed her hair.
As she gestured for me to wind down the window, I
turned towards HP.

"Just start the engine!" I hissed. "Reverse!"

"Why?" he asked. "What's going on?"

"I can't . . ."

She rapped on the window again, this time using her knuckles.

"Just roll down the window," said HP. "She'll put her fist through my glass if you don't."

I looked into my mom's face. She was a tidal wave, waiting to pour into the truck and fill up the space until we drowned. I held my breath and rolled down the window.

"Honey! I heard you two pull up and I just thought I'd come out and wish HP good luck."

"Good luck with what, Mrs. P?" His demeanor was so calm. He hunched forwards over the steering wheel, resting his chin on it.

"We'll be seeing a lot less of you for a while, I guess, because Angela won't be here. And about that—I just wanted to say that even if she's not around, you can still come over anytime and visit with me."

HP's face was a blank white sheet of paper, cut by moonlight.

"I'll keep that in mind, Mrs. P." He turned to me. "Roll that back up." He twisted the key in the ignition and threw the truck into reverse, leaving my mom standing in the driveway in her pom-pom slippers.

I should have told him earlier, maybe before the party, but I just hadn't found the right moment. He drove up the block to his house, which I wasn't expecting. He banged the door when he got out, and in two strides he was over by the old birch tree. I watched from the passenger seat as he pulled up the hood of his sweatshirt and slid his back down the bark of the trunk. After a minute I joined him. His house was dark except for one light still on in his parents' bedroom. Mrs. Parker always stayed up reading while her husband slept. HP and I sat in silence until he trod his flip-flop on top of mine.

"So, you're going somewhere?" he said.

My heart thumped. "I got into college. I leave next week. I was going to tell you. That's why I wasn't into the party. I was . . ."

He looked at me hard and then shook his head, laughing. "How far a drive, LJ? Or is it the community college in town?"

"England. Oxford University."

He put one hand flat on the top of his hood and pulled it forwards a few inches. Then he rubbed his face like he was washing it with soap. "When did you find out?"

"After grad weekend."

"Are you serious? Why didn't you tell me?" His voice sounded small. I felt desperate to hug him, to go lie down in his truck.

"I'm sorry. It's my parents. I don't want to go."

"Don't then. Don't go."

I put my hand on his arm, but he wouldn't look at me. "Can you come with me?"

The sound he made was sharp. "I don't think I'm Oxford material."

I looked down at my toes, curled them into my shoes.

"And you know I've got my own things going on. I've got the apprenticeship and I'm coaching the senior swim team." He pulled his hood farther down his face. "I just can't believe you wouldn't tell me."

We were quiet for a few minutes. The light in his parents' bedroom went out. When HP finally spoke again, his voice was softer.

"Look, it's good for you to go. You deserve it and . . . and you'll do well, I'm sure." He stood up and touched me on the top of the head.

I was fighting back tears, like a kid on the first day of kindergarten.

"So you'll have a blast. And it's only eight months. Jolly old England. Next time, tell me the truth, though, hey. And give me a bit of warning."

"But you don't get it. I'm only good when you're around. I don't know how I'm going to do this."

"I'll be here when you get back." He smiled. "It's not like I'm leaving town."

"Could you at least come visit?"

"Maybe. I'd need to save up. But, hey, maybe." An idea struck him and he brightened. "In the spring when coaching's done . . ." He counted off commitments on his fingers. "I'm sure my old man would give me a few weeks in April. Will you still be there? We could make it work." He held out his hand to me. His palm was dry and smooth when I took it.

"Really?" I asked.

"I'll try. And maybe Ez will come with me."

"Okay."

"Come on, I'll walk you home."

As we neared my old gray house, I said, "While I'm gone, don't hang out with my mother."

He shook his head. "Don't worry. The woman has fangs."

I laughed out loud, even through my tears. "Thank you," I said.

I'd never loved him more.

What do you mean it was none of my business?" my mother said in the morning, her steel-cut oatmeal cooling to the side of her. "I was inviting him to stay close to us as a family while you're gone. Can't you see it's going to be hard for him? Or do you only ever think of yourself?"

I slumped forwards on the breakfast bar. "I'm still not sure about going."

"Angela." She picked up her spoon and stirred the thick breakfast mush. "Sometimes we all have to do things in life that we find unsavory. Necessary things. I'm sorry you feel so stricken about HP, but I assure you he'll wait. You're a Petitjean. Girls like us aren't a dime a dozen, you know."

Those seven days until I flew to England, my insides were gripped by an invisible fist. HP and I packed as many lake swims and sunsets into the week as we could, but there was a melancholy to our conversations now. It was as if we'd read the final page of a chapter and could no longer concentrate on any of the words that preceded it.

On my last day in Cove, the phone rang.

"What?" said HP when I picked up.

"I didn't say anything."

"Sorry, I'm at work at the pool, everyone's shouting. Meet me at Fu Bar at six." He hung up with a click.

Even the bartenders at Fu Bar were underage. They all had high-fashion haircuts and wore orange flight suits unzipped to varying degrees. The bar was one of those aircraft hangar places, with aluminum pipe weaving all around the ceiling and hand-cut yam fries on the menu. No two chairs were alike, and all around on chalkboards were pithy quotes from movies. When I walked in at 6:20 p.m., the entire swim team was in the back room playing Ping-Pong and drinking pitchers of foamy pale ale. Ezra waved and strolled over.

"Little Miss Ivy League," he said, crooking his arm around my neck so that I stumbled forwards. "You were keeping that one quiet."

"I see you invited the guys. I never knew I was such good friends with them."

"HP's over there." Ezra gestured with his head towards the bar, where HP sat on a tall stool with his back against the counter, facing me. "He's been drinking since four."

HP still had his lifeguard whistle around his neck and his red board shorts on. Every so often his flip-flop would slide off the footrest of the stool, pitching him forwards. I headed towards him, and he sat up straighter in his seat and put his glass down, but before I could reach him a Jared-Jayden-Caleb-Kayden cut me off and swerved me towards the Ping-Pong table.

"You can be on my team!" he shouted. I didn't know his name. "Here, hold the paddle like this . . ." He hugged around me to adjust my grip, and I was hit by a waft of Axe deodorant. "Okay, we're playing first to twenty-one, you're on backhands."

I missed the opening serve because I was looking over my shoulder towards HP.

"Little John! Are you, like, one of those hot girls that suck ass at sports?"

"Allow me," said HP, arriving alongside the table and bumping the other guy off my team.

I looked up at the clean line of HP's jaw and the way his hair curled at his neck line.

He blinked hard and lifted his paddle into a kung fu stance. "Bring it."

I'm not sure how he even connected with the serve, but he blasted it back down the line, won the point and then put his paddle flat on the green of the table.

"Too easy. I need air. Coming?"

He put his arm around me and led us both to the back door of the pub. It felt fun, fluid, like this was the stream I was meant to be in, like I should never leave.

Outside we sat on some empty beer kegs. The brickwork smelled sour and the paving stones beneath our feet were tacky.

HP lifted his shirt and put a flat hand against his stomach. "I need food."

"You always need food," I said, chuckling, folding into his side, but he didn't absorb me. He was steep like a wall.

"Why haven't you kissed me properly at all this week? Is it because you're goddamn bullshit leaving? Because that means we should be kissing more, not less." He stabbed into the air with a determined finger. "Or have you got a fucking thing for Ezra?"

"HP, how drunk are you?"

"Three out of ten. Six, maybe."

"I couldn't kiss you properly because I'm sad."

"That's lame. You kissed me with your mouth all tight. Like a cat's ass kissing." He pointed at his lips, pursed and tense.

"HP!" I shoved him and he stumbled off the keg. "I don't know how to be." I smeared my palms on the thighs of my pants. "If I'm excited about going to Oxford, that's horrible because I'm leaving you. And if I dread Oxford, that's horrible because I'm going and I should make the most of it. That's what you always say."

HP burped and covered his mouth as he sat back down next to me.

"And meanwhile my parents are hovering behind my head, trying to implant every single feeling I have. I'm stuck. Aren't you? I mean"—I glanced at him carefully—"what do you want? Are we gonna be together while we're apart?"

"Depends. Are you in love with me?"

I pulled away from him. He held up both hands like a foiled bank robber.

"Hey, it's worth an ask."

Of course I was in love with HP, but if I told him now, would it matter? I'd always thought when I arrived at the moment of actually saying the sentence out loud, it would have more ceremony than a slimy beer patio with the guy swaying drunk.

HP let out a frustrated moan, loud and low like

a barn animal. "I'm gonna miss you. I'm gonna miss this."

My mother told me I should never kiss a boy if he's drunk, but I found myself moving towards HP's mouth, the taste of him smoky and raw. There was that flicker again as we slid into hunger, his hands tugging into my hair, both of us breathing fast as our hands moved over and under each other's clothes. I knew the ridges of him so well now, the grooves in his stomach and chest. I straddled his lap and he wrapped his arms all the way around me. Everything surrounding us fell away, irrelevant.

When we finally left the bar, the streets were empty. Our high school looked ghost-lit: one tennis ball sat in a drain out front. The Tastee Delite had closed shop and boarded its windows; NO KASH CEPT OVERNITE read the latest sign.

We drifted to his house and climbed into the back of his truck—we didn't even need to drive it anywhere. Above us, the stars glinted.

"Sometimes I think," said HP, bobbling my head on his chest with every word, "that the sky's just a dark blanket, and behind it is totally bright light. Those stars are just little pinprick holes in the cloth, letting us see what's behind." He sniffed. "See? I'm deep, too."

The crook of his neck smelled fresh, like a swimming pool. "I am in love with you. I just didn't want to say it with you shitfaced outside a bar."

He put his arm behind his head for a pillow. "I knew it."

"When I'm in Oxford, I'm not going to talk to any guys. Just so you know."

"Good."

"Are you going to talk to girls?"

He sat up. "I don't know, LJ, that's asking a lot. I mean, I can't make any promises. For instance, I might have to talk to my mom." We held hands, our fingers moving in and around each other's. "Listen." He bunched himself up to sit straighter. "I don't want you to spend the whole time thinking about me and Cove."

"I will, though."

"Well . . ." He shifted uncomfortably. "I'll be thinking about you, too, but we shouldn't be dating while you're away."

I stared at him hard.

"Wait. Fuck. I can't get words so they sound right." He spread his hands like a concert pianist. "Go to England and see what happens. I'll be here, *not* dating anyone. When you come home, we can see where we're at. Was that better? I think that went better."

"Are you in love with me?"

"Yes."

How was he always so certain of everything?

"Okay," I murmured. "We'll play it by ear. Like you'd ever stick to a plan anyway."

Together we slipped into exhausted sleep. When crows woke me the next morning, the pinprick stars were all gone. Clouds scuffed above me, their edges torn.

Detective Novak, I know all you want is to tick boxes on your checklist so you can close my file, but the truth of HP and me is more complex than anyone is allowing in here. What HP and I had was complete happiness. This isn't a love story. Or at the very least it's not *only* a love story. It's also a tale of utter reliance—*that's what you need to understand*. First. Before we move on.

You might think that everything I've told you just builds more of a motive for me to harm Saskia, but I'm innocent of whatever may or may not have happened to her. What I'm trying to say, Detective, is that HP had a hold on me. I needed him and I don't mind admitting that. I never felt as safe as when he was around. Of the coatrack versions of me, he always pulled out the best one, and if you're going to understand anything else I tell you today, you need to fully appreciate how much there was to lose if I lost him.

chapter

7

"Utter reliance?" Novak inspects his fingernails, polishes one with the soft pad of his thumb. "From what I've heard so far, your life is pretty darn swell. What would you have to worry about? Here's a girl at the top of her graduating class, who's beautiful—no, don't squirm—whose parents want nothing but the best for her and send her to an Ivy League college—*internationally*—to give her the greatest of starts. It doesn't really read like a sob story."

"My parents wanted the glory of a well-educated daughter. They wanted me to fly some kind of giant success flag for them. My needs didn't factor in, never have."

"You know what? I see a lot of kids come through this building that've been dealt rough cards, and believe me, you're not one of them."

"Detective Novak, just because I haven't witnessed the double homicide of my parents or had to eat out of dumpsters doesn't mean I don't know what's coming for me. We're all standing on the tracks."

"You're saying bad things happen to everyone?"

"Of course."

"Did something bad happen to Saskia?"

I ignore him. "Listen, my parents moved me around every couple of years, so I never had a real friend before HP. I'm trying to tell you why he was so important. My mom is . . . a glacier: she's cold and insidious. Little by little, she'll freeze you out and take everything you have."

He nods and begins to write. "What have you learned from your mother, Angela?"

I hesitate. "Honestly? I've learned that everything's a competition. And that everyone has an agenda even if they don't admit it."

"What's hers?"

"To push to the front. Climb to the top." There's a beat while Novak's still looking down at his page. "What's yours?"

He throws his pen onto the table in front of him. "I think my agenda's pretty straightforward, Angela."

"You say that, but everyone's hiding something."

"Are you?"

I look up at the crease where the wall joins the ceiling. "What I've come to understand about the world is that there are so few people in it who actually say what they mean." Novak wants to interrupt, but I don't present a gap. "I'm told it's because we're all being careful of one another's feelings, but that's not it. People don't say what they mean because they're deceptive. They're fake and they lie." My head hurts. "Novak, I'm just not good at lying or hiding. I'm honest to a fault, except I don't think it is a fault."

"Okay, so what you're telling me, Angela, is that despite a cushy life, you have an acute, at times paralyzing, fear of humanity's vulnerability. Without HP, you felt less able to cope with your own perception of a world full of liars. You needed his input to balance you out. Am I getting it?"

Surprisingly, he is.

He stands suddenly. "Wait here, I want to show you something." He returns carrying a small transparent bag, like the ones used for freezer food. He tosses it onto the table; I can see the tidy print of its label, the numerical code and a name. "Take a look."

I reach forwards and pull the bag towards me. There in the corner of the bag, hugged by the tight furrow of plastic, is a delicate silver necklace. Sitting above the folds of silver is a pendant, shaped like a tiny elephant, intricately patterned and colored in shades of festival blue. I feel my stomach hollow inward again, and struggle to breathe out.

chapter

8

"So, *honestly*, do you find the necklace upsetting? Is it Saskia's?"

I turn the bag over and look at the contents from the underside. There's a thickness in my throat that rises high before I can swallow it.

"You don't seem to be that concerned about this woman's disappearance. This is a missing woman from your town. You've talked and talked and talked. About yourself. You know Saskia, know her well, in fact—you've already admitted to that—and yet nothing you've said so far relates to her. Isn't that interesting?"

Nothing I say is understood. The man is a fool. I run a fingertip over the outline of the silvery-blue pendant.

He's watching my finger trace the shape. "There is something sad about that elephant, no?"

I shiver involuntarily and back away from the table. "Where did you find it?"

"Where do you think we found it?"

I shrug. Then he folds his hands neatly in his lap. "Why don't you tell me what happened at Oxford? Would you like that?"

"I would."

Do you know about Freddy Montgomery, Novak? Is he in my file? You must have stumbled across him during your investigation. There's no telling anything about Saskia unless I first tell you about Freddy. Freddy from Oxford. He knew the city by heart and he handed it over to me like a gift.

In the very center of the city there's a building called the Radcliffe Camera. It's pretty famous—you should Google it when you get home tonight. It's round and domed and inside is a library. On Saturday mornings I liked to go there, open a musty novel and settle against the curve of the wall while I looked out the window at the cobbled courtyard.

Everything outside that window is made of stone. An old church, silvered by centuries, looms over the entire square, and underfoot are slabs worn smooth by a million journeys. The Radcliffe Camera is set back a street from the commercial zone, but sometimes shoppers carrying bags filled with clothing and Apple products wander into the square as if arriving from the future.

It's quiet in the Rad Cam courtyard. There are a hundred rusty bikes, most with wicker baskets, parked against the black fence, and nobody steals them. And the Bodleian Library, one of the oldest libraries in the world, stands at the north end of the square facing Hertford College and the Bridge of Sighs, a windowed walkway that links two pale buildings in an upwards lilt unnoticeable to those drifting across it.

Hertford was my college. I hadn't expected to feel so at home in a new place, but when I arrived there mid-September and saw the gargoyles and statuesque heads along the top of the Bodleian wall and the numerous old bookshops, the blood in my body started to surge.

I'm sorry to hurt your true-blue Vermonter feelings, Detective Novak, but you must know by now I didn't feel any affinity with Cove. Oxford, though, oh, we clicked the minute I set foot in the place.

That day was the first time I walked through a door in a door. All the colleges have huge wooden gates that remain permanently closed, but the smaller doorways within them open and close, and can be locked with keys made from medieval iron. I'd never seen a door in a door before: it felt like a kid's book, where mice live in the baseboards. I rumbled my suitcase through the flagstone hallway of the porter's office and onto the hushed lawn of the quad, and there I stopped and sat down on my bag for a minute. Jet-lagged and out on my own, it struck me that I had never before been anywhere so perfect. Even the placards on the two benches bordering the lawn had been polished. Little windows to tutors' rooms sat just above the hedge line, fringed at the top by ivy, and to my left a winding stone stairwell led up to what I would discover to be the wood-paneled dining rooms of the college.

At first I didn't notice the young man standing in the archway across from me. It was only when he snapped his copy of *Crime and Punishment* closed that I looked over. He was leaning against the wall by the arches in studied contemplation, his dress shirt buttoned all the way to the tie that bulged at his neck.

"Hello there, good afternoon," he said, walking over and offering a moist hand. "I have to deduce that you're new to the college, judging by the size of your valise."

He was round and slightly pink.

"Can I help?" He pushed a signet ring around the base of his little finger. "It doesn't do to struggle up the stairs on one's own with a case twice the size of you."

I didn't consider myself that puny, and was about to reply when he spoke again.

"I'm Freddy. I'm sorry, do you actually speak English?"

"Do you always talk so much?"

"Gosh, no." He crossed his arms against his shirt, the stripes of which distorted at the midriff. His hair was cropped very close to his head, as if to preempt premature balding. "I rarely talk to newcomers. So you're American. What a relief. I was starting to think you were Eastern Bloc."

"I'm only half American. My grandfather was something European."

"Oh, crossbreeding—well played. Those Americans are everywhere, especially since we ship them in by droves to beat the bloody Cambridge lot in the boat race." He paused. I stared at him blankly. "The rowing? Gosh, you are a new girl."

Freddy never left my side the whole eight months I spent in Oxford. He was a third-year biochemist who'd also been to Magdalen College boarding school. That first day he took me to the Turf Tavern, a pub hidden away down a skinny alley I'd never have found on my own. The thirteenth-century beams over the bar were so low that even he had to bend at the knee while he ordered us half-pints of Speckled Hen.

"Some Australian prime minister set a Guinness

world record right where you're standing for quaffing a yard of ale." He passed a glass of swirling liquid back to me and prodded at the coins in his palm. "And that's all you need to know about that country."

We sat on a long oak bench with a red seat cushion that was worn into hard-packed lumps. Freddy chose a seat next to me, which made it hard to look at him. It felt like we were sitting in a train carriage. When he asked questions he rattled them out with the fear of someone racing the clock, as if a buzzer would sound somewhere and there'd be no more talking.

"And is there a gentleman currently with whom you are romantically engaged?" He ran a plump fore-finger around the rim of his beer glass.

I picked at the dark varnish on my nail. "There's a guy. But we're not dating while I'm here. We kind of are, but we're not."

"There's a guy, is there? Is he terribly handsome?"

"Most girls think so."

"Is he beefy? I bet he is. Who'd play him in a movie? And don't say that awful vampire chap or I'll be forced to abandon you."

"Harrison Ford."

"He's a hundred years old."

"When he wasn't." I took a wincing sip of the murky, warm Speckled Hen. "What about you, Freddy? Are you dating?"

"What a dreadful expression! From now on, we will not be using North American colloquialisms. Let's get some British into you! Come on, chin chin. We're off to the Ashmolean."

Freddy came with me to the opening ceremony of studies, where all new undergraduates had to parade through the streets of Oxford in gowns and mortarboards in order to listen to a don speak in Latin about our responsibilities as students. Beyond Freddy, I didn't bother to make any friends. Sure, I said hi when I passed people in the corridors of Hertford, and the porters all knew my name. But I didn't delve too deeply into the nightlife, or trawl for friends. It's never really been my thing.

From my college room, I could hear the rowdy bar crawls on Thursday nights and the weekend black-tie wanderers drinking from the necks of champagne bottles and shouting in plummy accents about kebabs. I never felt I was missing out. Freddy was somehow older than the average student—it was like he'd arrived at the university with all the refinement of a man in his late forties. He scorned what he termed "undergraduate thuggery" or the "yobs of college life." We went punting on the River Cherwell, and Freddy brought a wind-up 1930s gramophone. The only time we separated was to attend lectures and tutorials, but mine were few and far between and I barely prepared for them. Not having my dad around to check up on me felt like a whole new world. I exhaled into the absence of my mother. Finally I was a flower able to grow towards a different sun, in any direction I deemed fit.

As fall turned to winter, Freddy and I did things I could never do at home. It became my new challenge. We went brass-rubbing in Christ Church Cathedral, listened to fiery young politicians at the Union, saw plays touring from London at the Oxford Playhouse or took tea and crumpets at the Malmaison, talking about how a jail could fashion itself into a hip new hotel.

"What if you sleep in a murderer's old room? DNA persists, you know. It doesn't bear thinking about what might be on the pillows." He sighed and sipped his Earl Grey.

I did Skype with HP as often as I could, although the time difference made it difficult. His routine was fairly rigid, what with all the coaching and carpentry through the week, so we mostly spoke on weekends. The Parkers didn't have a laptop; all of our conversations took place at their computer in the kitchen, and often I could see the back of his mother as she stirred something at the stove or drifted past holding a bag of flour. HP struggled to figure out Skype and spent a lot of the calls pressing at buttons with his forehead too close to the camera. He'd cut his hair—shaved it down to a golden Velcro. His eyes and cheekbones dominated the screen.

"My dad said it was time I looked more like a carpenter than a surfer. Does it look bad?"

"Looking bad is genetically impossible for you."

"I miss you, LJ. How's the studying? Are you talking to any guys?"

"Not in that way, no." I didn't tell him about Freddy. Not because there was anything shifty about the friendship; just that over Skype, I worried Freddy's name would be a threat, when he was anything but. "I'm not working very hard," I offered instead. "But the city's amazing. I can't wait for you to come see it."

There was no set plan—as always with HP—but we talked of spring as if it were an anticipated reunion.

My mother didn't call much because it was expensive long-distance. We tried Skyping, but she spent most of the conversation disconcerted by her image on the screen and smoothing out her hair. Instead she wrote me emails. Her email account was petiteshelley@gmail.com, which made her sound like a teenage chat room user.

I've checked in your closet, she wrote, *and darling, you've left behind all of your prettiest clothes. Should I send them?*

Your dad wants to know if you've covered Virgil's "Aeneid" yet. I've no real desire to know what that is.

I hope you're eating in the Hertford College dining room. Pay as much attention as you can to the upper table, I've heard that's where all the dons sit.

It's only a matter of time, darling, before they all notice you. Remember how exceptional you are.

As well as relentless advice on forging a path into the upper echelons of Oxford society, Mom was also intent on giving me HP updates.

I saw him today going into the rec center—not with a girl, so don't worry!

And: *He's making quite a name for himself as a sports teacher.*

And: *HP has yet to come over for dinner. But I'm sure he will at some point.*

I didn't fly back home for Christmas—couldn't afford the ticket—and Mom said they weren't trying hard this year anyway. *What's the point, darling? It's not like we're Christians.*

I spent the holidays with Freddy at his home in Dorset. We took a taxi from the train station and drove up the long, meandering driveway through the grounds of his house, which turned out to be more of an estate. The front facade of the grand mansion boasted at least twelve windows. The cook, Esther, opened the door.

"Major and Mrs. Montgomery are in the conservatory. They said to freshen up and join them for tea."

The only thing missing from the scene was a butler.

Mrs. Montgomery was a thin, pinched woman with nostrils that seemed perpetually flared. She held out her hand and I hesitated, unsure if I should kneel and kiss it. The woman watched me for three days straight, barely cracking a smile, even on Christmas morning when we discovered that Freddy had put a book of British idioms and *An Idiot's Guide to Cricket* in my stocking.

"He's taking you on," his mother said from her silk armchair where she clasped a tray of crystallized ginger to her lap. Her face remained utterly without expression.

On Boxing Day, Freddy took me pheasant shooting with his father, a man with a formidable mustache and a seemingly bottomless silver flask of brandy from which we all had to drink every time we stopped.

"My son's rather taken with you," Major Montgomery said in a rare moment when Freddy was out of earshot.

"We're buddies," I said.

"Good heavens." He shook his head and snapped his shotgun open, crooking it over his forearm. "That'll never do."

I never found out if it was my inferior American phrasing he disliked or the platonic nature of my relationship with his son. When Freddy and I said goodbye to his folks in early January and prepared to return to Oxford, Mrs. Montgomery glared from the hallway while her husband shook my hand.

"Can we expect you next year?" he asked.

"She'll be back with the Yanks by then," chirped Freddy.

Both his mother and father exhaled visibly.

The strangest thing about Christmas, aside from the austerity of Freddy's parents, was spending it without HP, but I got back to Hertford to find he'd sent me his version of a festive postcard. On the front of the card was a photo of the Cove library, as if it were some kind of heritage landmark, and HP had cut out a picture of Santa in the mall from the local paper and stuck it to the back of the card. Around the picture, in writing getting progressively smaller as he ran out of room, he'd written *Merry Xmas from Cove, cultural hotspot. Dumping snow here, working hard, miss you in my truck. Fly back to me soon, little free bird.* I stuck it to the pinboard above my desk.

As the months passed towards spring, we Skyped less. He was busy finishing up his year of coaching, or perhaps his dad was working him hard. I stayed busy with Freddy, fighting through hordes of Japanese tourists around St Giles' and taking sardonic tours of the city in an open-top double-decker bus, Freddy disagreeing with everything the tour guide said on the loudspeaker.

It was a relief when a second postcard arrived from HP in April with a picture of the Hulk smashing something on the front. In HP's scrawl was a single sentence, *Hey gray eyes, check your windows.* I had no idea what he was referencing until the night of April 30, when I woke to a scattering of small pebbles hitting my window at four o'clock in the morning and looked out to see HP and Ezra on the street below Hertford College.

Detective Novak holds up a palm like a policeman halting traffic.

"Your friends. They're always male." He checks his watch. "Don't you find that interesting?"

"Like I said, I've always been a bit on the outside of things, and if a friend comes my way, it feels lucky."

"So Freddy replaced HP on that trip? It seems like a pretty straight trade."

"Are you psychoanalyzing me or something?"

Novak's eyebrows shoot up. "It's my job to ask questions, Angela."

"I thought your job was to listen."

Novak's lucky I'm even talking to him. I could have clammed up from the very start, but I'm doing this for HP, who might well be going through hell right now. I'm doing this for him and for me: the truth is I've bottled up this travesty for years.

I missed HP desperately while I was at Oxford and there's no way Freddy could replace him. I remember the immediate calm that came over me when I saw HP standing below the college holding a flower from the hydrangea bush.

"Can we crash?" he shouted.

"What are you doing?" I laughed. "Wait there." I hurried to find a robe, stopping in front of the mirror for a second to pinch my cheeks and check my hair. After a quick scrub of toothpaste across my teeth, I jogged to the college gate, pushing open the tiny door and stepping through it onto the street. My body wasn't fully through before HP grabbed me and swept me into a hug. His neck smelled like summer. He set me down and bent to look properly at my face.

"You any different?"

I'd cut my hair shorter, pixie-style, and I knew with the light from the streetlamp my cheekbones looked good. HP walked me around in a circle, giving me short, tentative kisses that pecked like questions. *Are we still the same? Have the rules changed? Is this still as good as before?* We didn't have time to find out because Ezra cut in.

"We got free bourbon on the plane!" he announced. "That stewardess kept it flowing. I think she kind of dug us. Shitty movies, though."

"Why didn't you tell me you were coming?"

"You didn't get my postcard?" HP looked crestfallen.

"Dammit! I laid off Skype just to set up the mystery. You didn't get it?"

"Did you put a date on it, bonehead?" asked Ezra, slapping HP with his cap.

"Does today work for you?" HP took my hand and laid his squashed hydrangea into it, closing my fingers. "Come on, let's stash our gear and you can show us the town."

As it turned out, they'd picked the best daybreak of the year to arrive in Oxford. It was May Morning, a traditional celebration that had been going for over five hundred years, and every student in town was heading to Magdalen Bridge to hear the Hymnus Eucharisticus sung from the towers by boy choristers. The university year was coming to a close, and all the colleges would throw a grand May Ball to round out the celebrations. As we walked down High Street towards the Botanic Garden, the roads started to fill with bicycles. Some students hadn't been to bed all night—you could tell from the haunted faces above the stripy scarves. HP and Ezra kept stopping to look up at buildings.

"You've got to be kidding me," HP said every twenty steps. "The walls have gargoyles. That's ridiculously cool."

They were jet-lagged, both of them, and fighting the fade, but the birds twittered in hedgerows as we walked past the Eastgate Hotel. The sky held a cobalt promise. At the bridge a crowd stood expectantly, their faces raised to the tower.

"What are we looking for?" Ezra yawned.

"Wait for the chimes." I had both hands in my jacket pockets, but HP reached in and laced his fingers through mine. His hair had grown by a couple of inches and sat in a tousled scruff. He looked up like everyone else, but he had that familiar golden glint at his jawline and I pressed into him until he put his arm around me. I could feel the strength of his stomach through the lining of his clothes. I felt settled, happy, as if there'd been parts of myself I hadn't known I'd missed until he brought them back for me. With the first strike of six from the clock tower, everything else fell silent. The boys looked down at me for a moment, only to swing their faces back skyward as the Magdalen College Choir broke into hymn, as they'd done on that day for more than five centuries. We all stood still listening to blackbirds and boy sopranos; even Ezra looked reverent.

At 6:10 a.m. the singing ended and the bells rang out of Magdalen Tower. People cheered and hugged as Morris folk dancers appeared on the street with bells tied to their elbows and ankles, and drunken students climbed the bridge to jump into the river—only to think twice when they saw the water level. Ezra turned to HP and me.

"This place rules," he shouted, joining a band of

dancers, heel-toeing his way into the line and leaving me alone with HP for the first time in months. It didn't take us long to curl into a kiss. I arched up and he leaned down and as the crowd bumped us we rediscovered the feel of each other. It felt like a wedding, the kiss on the steps outside the church with a frenzy of bells and cheering. HP broke off to catch his breath—his face was familiar but shy somehow.

"Have you been having a good time here?" He had to yell above the din.

"I love it here," I said.

"Yeah? I told you so. You sticking around?" I knew he was hedging; he really only had one question.

"Till the end of the semester. Only two more weeks!"

He brushed a dark strand of hair from my forehead. "So, will we . . ." he began, but behind us a new voice cut in.

"Angela Petitjean, as I live and breathe!"

Of course it was Freddy. I'd promised to meet him at the bridge and had forgotten the plan in all the excitement. He wore a tweed blazer and cream chinos, one pant leg tucked into a paisley sock so as not to get bike oil on it. Under his arm was an umbrella.

"I thought I might find you here. That hymnus was glorious, although the tenors lacked conviction." He glanced at HP. "Who's this?"

The words tumbled out quickly. "Freddy, this is HP. HP, Freddy."

A light dawned on Freddy's face. He held out his right hand, the fingers and thumb closed and rigid. "The guy. What a pleasure. Now tell me, are you named after the sauce or the computer company?"

HP shook Freddy's hand.

"Or perhaps you're Harry Potter?"

"I don't read kids' books."

"Not even as a child, I'll warrant." Freddy's head tilted.

HP took a breath to say something but at that moment Ezra arrived back from dancing. "English girls, man, they know how to party. Holy cow. Oh, hey." He held his right hand up for a high five. "How's it going?"

Freddy stared at Ezra's palm.

"Ez, this is Freddy." I lowered Ezra's arm for him. "He's a biochemist."

"I'm sorry to hear that, dude. But I guess somebody has to be."

HP chuckled.

"I'm taking these guys to go get breakfast on Cowley Road," I hurried. "You want to join us, Freddy?"

"I'd be delighted." Freddy's eyes glittered towards HP. "After all, celebrity guests deserve the best Oxford experience. Angela and I can fill you in on what's what."

Freddy bowed his head and linked his arm through mine, pushing us forwards into the throng while the boys followed behind. When I strained back through a gap over Freddy's shoulder, I could see HP trudging with his hands in his jean pockets while Ezra wove in and out of groups of long-haired girls drinking champagne straight from the bottle.

Café Coco was teeming even though it was barely seven in the morning. We slid into the last available booth. The room was divided into two halves, split by an art deco bar where a sleepy-eyed waiter lolled a cocktail shaker close to his right ear. Behind the bar was a sculpture of a man sitting in a large porcelain bath. Our table was bare, save for a porcelain egg cup filled with rough clumps of brown and white sugar. While HP and Ezra stared at Freddy, I peered for ages at the specials on the blackboard, glancing back now and again at each of their uneasy faces.

"Mimosa, Ange?" piped Freddy after a long pause. "I think it'd be rude not to."

"I'm in. Guys, do you want one?"

"Is it a beer?" asked Ezra. "It better be."

Freddy's cell phone began to ring in his blazer pocket. "It's champagne and freshly squeezed orange juice." He rummaged for his phone and stared down at the number on the screen as he wriggled out of the booth. "Do excuse me, chaps. Back in a mo'."

We watched him scurry to the back of the café and push through the doors towards the bathrooms.

HP pulled his hoodie off over his head, taking three-quarters of his T-shirt with it. He rearranged himself but wouldn't look at me. "You two seem close."

"He's my friend. He's been kind to me."

"Oh, I bet he has." HP nodded over at the waitress, and when she arrived at the table he ordered three beers. "And what's good to eat? Everything you have is made with goat's cheese."

"You don't like goat's cheese?" She curled a strand of blond hair for him, jutting a hip out and slanting her chrome tray against it. "It's really smooth and creamy."

I rolled my eyes. "Just bring us the beers, okay? I'll help my friends with the menu."

She returned a few moments later, looking only at HP as she slid the bottles onto the table.

He took his and raised it. "Here's to the real people."

The three of us clinked.

Freddy came back from the washrooms but didn't sit down again. His nose wrinkled at the sight of us drinking, because he found distasteful either the beer or the fact we were drinking it without glassware.

"A word, if I may." He raised his eyebrows at me. "It was very nice meeting you, gentlemen. Enjoy the mother country; I'm sure Ange will show you the best bits."

HP and Ezra tilted their bottles to him with their mouths pressed closed.

Once we were huddled in the yellow doorway of the café, Freddy gripped my wrist.

"Do you seriously expect me to believe that *that* is the guy?" He threw furtive glances back at HP, who was in the booth with Ezra, both of them laughing. "Angela, they're . . . they're children! You're miles beyond them."

"What's it to you?"

He blinked at me for a few seconds and let go of me, quietly hooking his umbrella over his forearm.

"That call was from Keble College. They have our May Ball tickets." Freddy adjusted the tuck of his handkerchief in the pocket of his blazer. "I took the liberty of ordering two more for your . . . friends. I assume they're staying? I'm off to pick the tickets up now."

"Thanks."

He sighed and reached out for my forearm again, gentler this time. "You can do what you wish, of course. Romance-wise, I mean."

"You think you know me, Freddy?" I pushed forwards off the window and pulled the café door open. "I'm miles beyond you, too."

I watched as the hurt unfurled in his eyes like squid ink through water. He turned on his heel and clipped briskly away down Dawson Street.

Ezra wanted to do typically tourist things while he was in Oxford, so we spent days punting on the Isis, or visiting the arts cinema in Jericho where Ezra refused to read the subtitles and spent hours throwing popcorn at the prettiest girls. As much as I liked the joviality of Ez, I was getting tired of him fast. In my college room, HP and I shared my single bed, but with my arm outstretched I could literally touch Ezra's knee as he lay on the floor. Every time we tried to whisper in the darkness, Ezra either shushed us or joined the whispering. Finally HP and I carved out some time for just us, and I took him to my favorite haunt.

HP slowed as we reached the courtyard of the Radcliffe Camera, where the sky was cloudless behind the dome. He stood with his hands on his hips, staring up at the glass and masonry as I sat down on the broad step of the Bodleian Library, my back against the door.

"Amazing, hey?"

HP turned. "It looks different every time I see it. Maybe it's the color of the sky." He sat down next to me.

"Are you having fun?"

"I am." He nodded slowly. "You?"

"Good. I'm great. Listen, I wanted to thank you for coming over. I haven't had a chance to say that yet."

"You're welcome."

Our words felt formal, like we were interviewing

each other for a corporate job. In the three days that had gone by, we'd rarely spoken of home.

"So how's Cove? Anything to report?"

"Coaching's good. Carpentry's good. But you know Cove. Nothing ever happens." He kicked the heel of one shoe against the step. "Especially compared with here."

"What do you mean by that, exactly?"

"I don't know—I just feel like you're . . ." He took a breath. "Do I need to worry about this Freddy guy?"

"Oh, God, no," I said. "There's nothing going on with me and Freddy. Seriously, the guy irons his jeans so there's a pleat down the front." I pulled HP's arm so he rocked closer. "I didn't tell you about him because I didn't want you to worry."

"Look, it's all good and I believe you and everything. Just . . . don't lie to me, LJ. I can't stand liars."

"Freddy's just a friend. I swear to God."

"Okay," he said, kissing me quickly. "Enough about Freddy. Enough." He looked out over the courtyard, where the tourists were making peace signs for photos. "So are we together still? Or are we 'seeing what happens'?"

"Don't ask me! You were the one who wanted to make it vague in the first place." It came out sharper than I'd intended, and I saw his eyebrows knit again.

I slipped my arm through his. "I think we should stop worrying and just relax back into each other."

"Yeah." He stretched and ruffled his hair. "Yeah, let's just have some fun. Good call. Enough of all this heavy shit." He pulled me towards him by the neck of my T-shirt.

We kissed as we stood, surrounded by tourists and pigeons and the singsong bells of bicycles. We couldn't get to my college room fast enough.

That night we drank in the bars on Cowley Road and partied in the O2 nightclub. It was full of synthetic smoke and weird lighting that gave all the clubbers blue teeth and dandruff. We hadn't checked ahead so it was some kind of jungle DJ who played music so manic, it made me feel like I was about to have a panic attack. I retreated to the back bar where the beat was reduced to a dull thump and let the boys get on with it.

At around 2 a.m. we wandered back up Cowley Road, stopping at Kebab Kid for the boys. The puddles shone psychedelic with grease. I waited outside, sitting on a nearby bus shelter bench, and stared at an old man in the doorway of a betting shop. He'd vomited on the front stoop and couldn't get up from it—every few minutes he'd skid his toe forwards looking for a foothold before slumping back against the door.

A guy with a foot-high Afro loped along the sidewalk asking everyone he passed for money. His hips led his stride, his gait spongy. If denied money, he'd point in the person's face and say, "Fuck you." He moved through the whole late-night crowd that way, repeating his script until, by the fifth attempt, he simply said, "Can you spare some change fuck you," all in a single breath. Wherever you looked on Cowley Road there was humanity, the true slimy viscera of it.

And yet there was HP through the smeary kebab shop window. There he was, pointing at sauces, jostling and joking, befriending everyone standing around him. I watched him from ten feet away, loving him for his knack of happiness. He was a rarity, a resilient light, and with a world full of choices surrounding him, he continued to choose me.

chapter

9

"I'm curious, why did HP bring his friend to England with him?" Novak interrupts my daydream. "I mean, here's a guy who's crazy about a girl, saves up all his money to come see her after a prolonged absence . . . and brings his buddy along. Doesn't that strike you as odd?"

I keep my face still. "HP and Ezra were a double act back then. They did a lot together."

"Perhaps he wanted a buffer." Novak sits forward, his eyes sharp. "Did you ever think about that?"

If he's trying to get a rise out of me, he'll have to do better.

"No? Okay. Just asking." He stands suddenly and pushes back his chair along the squeaking linoleum, then drifts around the table with his hands in his pockets and stares out the thin horizontal window that flanks the right side of the room. He seems to be whistling through his teeth.

"I'm sorry, am I boring you?" I ask.

He doesn't turn. "You have a rather pessimistic view of the world." On the way back around the table he hesitates, and instead pulls out the chair next to mine and stands in the gap.

I feel like a Catholic at a confessional, the priest joining me in the booth.

Novak sits down in the chair, facing me. "Do you think it's normal that Saskia's missing? Is it all just part of life's inescapable loss?"

I ignore his question. "Do you watch safari shows, Novak? I watched this show on Discovery once where a mom hippo and her baby were trying to cross a river, and this other grown male hippo comes in and starts stomping the riverbed so that the mom and baby get separated."

Novak breathes heavily.

"They were crying for each other, the mother and the baby. It is the rawest noise I've ever heard. The adult hippo stamped the baby to death while the mom was forced to stand and watch." I let that sink in. "That's nature at work; that's natural. Animals understand the imminence of danger, and yet they still bond. I find that interesting."

Novak scratches his cheek. "It seems you'd like to educate people on how to behave."

He's starting to invade my space. I fight the urge to push my chair away from him. "I'm just saying we should all admit it: there's always sorrow. It's why we're here right now, Novak."

He shakes his head. "So, which hippo are you in that story?"

"Which hippo? That's your question?"

"The male one?"

"Please. I'm talking about my worldview, not playing pretend."

He pauses, meters his words like a metronome. "Did you hurt Saskia to prove a point?"

"No."

He scribbles a few more words, underlining something, pressing hard. When he speaks again his voice is too breezy. "Well, I'm sorry I cut into your story. I hope you haven't lost your thread. So . . . HP and Ezra joined you at Oxford. Didn't you all attend some kind of ball?"

He's been talking to HP. I nod imperceptibly.

"What did you wear to the ball, Angela?"

I let out one bark of a laugh. "How's that relevant?"

"Good storytelling's in the details. You know that."

"I wore a men's white dress shirt, tailored so it fit. It stopped at my thighs. I had on a black necktie, worn loose, and heavy mascara. Black knee-high boots. Four-inch heels."

He pulls at the knot of his tie, loosening it. "See? That tells me a lot."

"Such as?"

"You grew up. You finally figured out you were attractive. And you wanted HP to realize it."

We stare at each other across the table. I can play this game, too, if he wants.

chapter
10

When I clipped down the stairs to the Hertford quad in my high heels, HP and Ezra were waiting on the lawn in their tuxedos. They both turned and bowed. I'd never seen either of them look so grand. HP's tux fit the line of his shoulders perfectly, and the white of his high collar made his face look even more tanned. He'd been to the barber's, his hair cut close to his neck and parted to the side like Robert Redford as Jay Gatsby. Ezra had shaved.

For weeks I'd practiced walking in my boots up and down the wooden floor of my college room. Of course I didn't attempt the grass, but my steps were confident as I strode along the stone path to its edge.

"You look . . . like, wow." HP headed towards me.

"That's a hell of a long way from your T-shirt at grad," added Ez with a whistle. "Hey, you don't get any offers tonight, you can totally come home with me."

"M'lady," said HP, ignoring his friend.

I took HP's arm and together we headed out of the gates of Hertford towards Keble, stealing glances at each other every now and again. The electricity between us crackled with every step. Detective Novak, it was the best ten minutes I'd had in Oxford.

Freddy stood at the main entrance in a waistcoat and tails. When we were ten steps away from reaching him, HP suddenly grabbed me around the waist and pressed me to the rusty college brickwork.

He kissed me full on the lips. "Let's have an epic night."

I wasn't usually one for public displays of affection but honestly, I could have ditched the entire ball and just gone back to my room with HP right there and then.

"Ladies and gents." Freddy arrived at our side, his eyes darting. "I hate to push in, but if we don't hurry all of the champers will be gone." He stretched in past HP's chest and kissed me on the cheek. "You're looking enchanting, my darling. I'm reminded of *A Clockwork Orange*."

"Good." In heels I was exactly Freddy's height.

"Shall we?" He flourished us towards the entrance,

and we all trailed through the grandeur of the main doors together. Keble's quad is six times the size of Hertford's, and they'd jammed it full of every fun activity imaginable. With the college buildings as a parameter, the inner lawns thudded with music. We stood, wide-eyed, looking at the spread.

To the left of us was a huge beer tent, nudged to the right by bumper cars rented from the carnival. They'd set up a greasy pole in the very center of the quad for students to straddle while they hit one another with pillows, and next to that was a bungee rope that you had to run hard and fast away from in a Velcro suit, only to be whipped backwards and stuck to a wall like a bug on flypaper.

We didn't know where to start.

"I vote beer," shouted Ezra above the din. He and HP headed through the flaps of the white marquee, leaving me standing alone next to Freddy. He put his arm around me.

"Have you been enjoying your week, Ms. Petit-jean?" His teeth blushed from too much Malbec. He must have started early.

"It's been fine." I put one hand on his lapel. "Listen, I'm sorry I was a bitch to you at Coco's."

"Oh, pish-posh. Let's not bother with piffle."

"But you've been kind to me, Freddy. From the very start."

"Well, you're special, my darling. Not everyone's as brilliant and unkind as you are."

I turned to see if he was joking and felt relieved when he trumpeted his nose into his spotted handkerchief. "Come on. We're wasting time. Let's go and find the champers."

Inside the beer tent, it was even louder and the walls shone slick with heat. We spied HP and Ezra by the bar and started to push our way through the bodies towards them. I slipped under the elbow of a man in a white dinner jacket and popped up into the middle of the boys' conversation. HP was roaring with laughter and a girl in a sky-blue, skintight dress was touching her hand onto his forearm as if to say, *Stop it immediately, I can't take any more of your fun.*

"I'm serious," Ez was yelling. "We got home with no shirts and a black eye each and his mom took photos of us."

The girl shook her head, the locks of her blond hair tickling at her bare shoulders. She was slim, wore very little makeup and had freckles across her nose and a strange, dark tan on the bottom half of her face that made it look like she'd dipped her chin in cocoa.

"You guys are awesome." I could hear she was Australian.

"Hey." I inched myself into the outer curve of the circle. "Did you get me a drink?"

Ezra and HP looked sideways at each other.

"I'll go," said Ezra. "What are you having?"

I stepped with Ezra to the bar, looking back over my shoulder distractedly to see HP hunker down and listen to something else the girl was saying. When he replied he covered his mouth with his hand to make sure he didn't spit on her. He only did that when he was making an effort.

"LJ!" Ezra poked me in the back with a stubby finger. "What are you drinking?"

"Champagne. And one for Freddy. Who's the girl?"

"She's an Aussie, just back from the Alps; some kind of snowboard instructor."

When he handed me two glasses of champagne, he shoved them and they spilled a little. He wiped his fingers down his lapels and hurried back into the circle. Freddy stood behind me and reached over to take his glass.

"Bloody Australians," he said into my ear. "Who wears flip-flops to a ball?"

I glanced at the girl's feet and headed back into their circle.

"Why's your face half brown?" I asked. HP, Ezra and the girl turned to me.

"Spring skiing," chorused the boys.

119

"What's with the tattoo?" I nodded at her left forearm, the inside of which was inked with an elephant, decorative and colored.

"Elephants are heaps beautiful. They keep soul mates for life and mourn their loved ones." Her teeth blazed whiteness. She looked like she ate nothing but apples. "And I like their knees."

I snorted.

"Little John, we're going out to do the bungee run. You in?" HP drained his pint glass.

"God, no."

"Little John? Cool name! Like the Merry Men!" The true blue of the girl's eyes shone. "So which one of you is Robin Hood?"

HP and Ezra both pointed to their own chests.

"What's your name?" I fired back.

She held out a smooth, toned arm. "I'm Saskia."

When I shook her hand her fingers felt icy against mine.

At the mention of Saskia, Novak sits up straight in his chair.

"Look at you," I say. "It's the arrival of Saskia into my story. You must be excited."

He knocks his pen against the clipboard on his knee. "I was interested to know how your paths first crossed. And more interested in hearing how they led you here."

"Hey, I'm only here for another . . . sixteen hours. Give or take. Beyond that, my path splits."

He tilts his head. "You must have hated her tattoo. Elephants have soul mates? I thought you had the monopoly on those."

"Between you and me, Novak, I wouldn't take anything Saskia tells you to be well researched."

He laughs once, but I know what he's doing. He's pretending to be on my side.

"Okay, so here's Saskia, moving in on your guy. If this was a love story, we would have reached the problem stage."

"That's funny." I don't smile. "In any story, Saskia is the problem stage."

I only watched the bungee rope for a few minutes. Saskia went first, of course, and the sight of her sprinting in that stretchy dress was enough to send me back to the beer tent. When the barman bent down to wash some glasses, I swiped an open bottle of champagne, two-thirds full, and headed out into the quad with it. The grass was already getting mulchy along the sides of the lawn and I teetered along it, trying not to slide in my boots.

Every few meters around the inner courtyard of Keble small stone stairwells led up to offices, probably rooms for tutorials or dons' chambers. Like everything in that hallowed city, the stairwells were made of stone, and since there were no gaps in the railing I could sit at the top of the steps with my back against the locked chamber door, completely hidden from the crowd.

I climbed up one of the staircases and paused at the top, looking out from the ivy-covered balcony above the party. Now that Saskia had finished her turn, she stood to the side with HP. She'd tied her hair up into a knot at the back of her head: sun-bleached ends splayed outwards from the center like a firework. She was breathing heavily as she poked HP in the ribs; he stood with his arms crossed, grinning and watching Ezra strap into the bungee.

The sky had darkened. It seethed above me in slashed indigo; only a few stars persisted. I grasped the champagne bottle to my chest and slid down the blue paint of the door behind me, letting my legs slump in front of me on the step. The champagne bottle clinked against my front tooth as I sucked down the fizzy froth. It wasn't long before Freddy found me. He jogged up five of the ten steps and then hesitated.

"What are you doing?"

"Getting wasted. What does it look like?"

"Can I join you, or . . ." His hands rested uncertainly on the thick of his hips, his tux pushed back. He looked like a penguin.

I smacked the step with an open palm, and once he'd puffed up the rest of the stairs to the doorway next to me, I passed him my champagne bottle. He took a small swig and grimaced.

"It's mostly backwash by now," I muttered.

"Delightful." He brought his knees up to his chest and laced his hands around them. "So who are we hiding from up here? The madding crowd, the Australian or Harrison Ford?"

"It's a toss-up," I hissed.

"Let her know who's boss if he means this much to you."

"She's beautiful."

"She's pretty. If you're unimaginative."

I thumped my head against the wooden door. "It's not meant to go like this."

I peered over the wall of the balcony. I couldn't see HP or Saskia, but Ezra was on the greasy pole hitting a skinny boy with a pillow. Where the hell had the other two gone?

"Life doesn't always go to plan," Freddy said.

"People like us, Freddy." I stood and took two steps towards him. "We can have it *all*." I pushed down his knees and straddled his thighs as he blinked up at me. "Wouldn't you say thasstrue?" I knew I slurred the question. I didn't care.

"Angela . . ." Freddy turned his face away from mine.

"You seriously don't want this? Tell the truth," I whispered into his ear, kissing his neck. My nails raked the back of his head.

When I reached down and felt into his crotch, he whimpered, "You don't want this," although his fat hips were starting to grind into my thighs.

For a minute I rode there on his lap as the skin around his collar reddened and his breathing turned to gasps. His hands grabbed at my breasts and he pinched a nipple, grunting, "Angela," his eyes squeezed tight in pleasure, "you're the only—" and it was then that I stopped. I pushed back and stood, staring down at him as he squirreled and heaved in the doorway.

"You've been lying to yourself, Freddy. I can't stand liars."

I turned and walked down the stairs.

At the base of the stairwell I'd almost finished straightening my clothes when I heard HP's voice.

"Where've you been?" He was alone. He'd unbuttoned his collar, and his bow tie hung loosely around his neck.

"Nowhere." I smoothed my bangs flat.

"I've been looking all over for you."

124

"No you haven't."

"Little John, listen . . ." His brow was furrowed. "I wasn't doing anything wrong."

"Except flirting with that dumb Australian. Her face is half tanned."

"I'm not flirting. She's fun, that's all." He wiped one hand against the other. "Hey, we never said we weren't allowed to h—" He stopped then and stared at the steps behind me.

I turned to see Freddy walk down the last of the stairwell, tucking his shirt into the front of his pants and tugging down his waistcoat. Freddy stood still when he saw us and I wheeled back to face HP.

"Wait." I took a step towards him.

"You were up there with *him*?"

"It's not how it looks." I reached for his arm, while behind me Freddy piped up.

"Excuse me," he said, like a keynote speaker. "Don't badger her, please. It's unbecoming."

"Get fucked, Professor Plum." HP pulled his tie off and stuffed it into his pocket. "Nobody's buying your *we're just friends* act. As *if* you don't want to get with her."

Freddy's face crinkled like there was a smell. "*Get with her*? Good Lord. What on earth happened to the English language when it traveled across the pond? It's been nothing but a steady decline. *Get with her.*" He sighed theatrically.

HP took a stride towards Freddy, who backpedaled, bracing one hand against the thickness of the banister, but instead HP grabbed my arm and turned me a half step. "Wow, LJ, talk about making a guy feel better about things. Were you hooking up?"

"Was *I* . . . ? No! Were *you*?" I shouted. "I mean, get all outraged if you like, HP, but let's just have a think for a minute about where *you* were. 'Play it by ear,' you say, 'let's just go with the flow' "—I knew my face was vicious—"and then you ignore me for the whole of our biggest night in Oxford and wander off with some random fucking Australian who's clearly hitting on you. How am I supposed to feel?"

HP looked at me like I'd grown a second head. "I was being friendly! Jesus Christ, hang a guy for wanting to have some fun. You know what you are, LJ? Jealous and clingy." He daggered a look at Freddy. "And shady with friendships." He stalked away through the mud towards the beer tent.

I watched the back of him until he was gone.

"I'm not shady."

Freddy readjusted his waistcoat, shaking his head at me. He didn't reply. A moment later he'd gone, too.

chapter

11

Novak glances at the clock on the wall. "That was cruel."

I shrug. "Which part?"

"You toying with Freddy like that. The boy was clearly in love with you."

I shake my head, sighing. "You're not very good at spotting villains, are you?"

"You don't know me well enough to tell." He's pleased with that one. "Has it occurred to you that HP might not be your Prince Charming? The way I remember it, Prince Charming stays all night by his true love's side, enraptured by her, lavishing her with attention, searching high and low for her when she vanishes. Yours didn't even buy you a drink."

I shift in my chair. "It was Saskia's fault. If she hadn't shown up, the whole evening would have been different."

"And yet you say you're not building a motive." He writes something down.

"Motive for what?"

He pretends he hasn't heard. "I wonder if Lacy wishes you hadn't shown up at the grad party."

I frown. He pulled that one out of nowhere. "That was different."

"Sure, okay." Novak looks up. "So, is this where your lifetime of hating Saskia began? Oxford?"

"I never said I hated her. I said she was a thief."

"Did you see her again before you left town?" He's like the keen kid in the front row of the movie theater now. Suddenly my story's top billing.

"No. Ezra called from the airport. I could hear his husky voice dwarfed by beeps and announcements over loudspeakers. HP wouldn't speak to me."

"How does that link to Saskia?"

"Take a guess, Detective."

"She was at the airport, too?"

It's tiring having to go through this again. It was hard enough the first time. "Wow," he says. "Talk about crashing the party."

It's almost like he finally gets it. I hear something buzz along his belt line. He's wearing a pager? Who uses those anymore?

Novak stands up and glances at the screen. "We need a break. Can I get you a snack, or coffee? Milk? Sugar?"

"Plain black is good, thanks."

When he reaches the door, he turns. "Don't go anywhere."

Very funny. Novak leaves me alone in this room again, the blink of the video camera the only sign of life. I grab both granola bars Novak brought at the very start and eat one after the other, dropping the wrappers onto the floor.

When he returns, he's not carrying the promised coffee. He has a bundle of letters that he sets on the table, facedown, so only the cream backs of the envelopes show. He pinches his suit pants up at the thigh before he sits, choosing his normal side of the table.

"The May Ball wasn't the last you ever saw or heard from Freddy Montgomery?" This question feels weighted: Novak's holding his breath.

"Is that what you have there? The letters Freddy wrote me after?"

"Can you generalize what most of these letters were about?"

"Why?" I wait for a beat. "They're right there. You've read them."

"I suspect he wrote you more than what I have here." Novak thrums the ten or so letters with his fingernail. "You can tell me this isn't a love story, but I think Freddy Montgomery might beg to differ."

I feel myself blushing. "They're not love letters. Not really."

"Who wrote the first one?" He's looking me in the eye a lot since he returned.

"Me. I wrote to say sorry for being a crappy friend." Why is he so interested in Freddy?

Novak eases a fatter letter from the file, takes his time unfolding it.

"*Dear Angela*," he begins. "*Most certainly you are welcome at my place next weekend—I think by now we can both assume the invite's ongoing.*" Novak stops reading. "What's he talking about?"

"His apartment. In New York. He has a nice apartment there."

"I thought he was British."

"Sometimes British people decide not to live in Britain."

The muscle in Detective Novak's jaw tightens. "We know he's big in chemical weaponry. Biochemistry made him rich."

"You've done your Googling. Yes, he's a millionaire. He can buy apartments wherever he wants."

He goes back to reading out loud. "*I'd invite you to*

130

a 'work do' I have on the Saturday, only it'll be filled with dreadful bores who'll spend the evening quoting opinions they've read in the New York Times, *trying to pretend they're their own."* Novak stops. "What is it about you two that you think you're smarter than everyone else?" Novak tosses the letter back to the table, where it spins for a second on the chrome. "Haven't you ever met your match?"

"Not so far." Novak's eyes bore into my face. "Detective, you can't seriously think Freddy's involved in this. He barely knows Saskia."

"He hates her, though, by default." Novak stabs the bottom of the letter on the table. "What does this mean? *Good luck navigating the unimaginative people.*"

"He always signs off with that. Cross-reference the other letters, if you haven't already." I glance up at the window. "Freddy understands me."

"How much imagination does it take to orchestrate a homicide, do you think, Angela? Surely there's a lot of planning."

"*I* wouldn't know."

"Did you two come up with a plan to show the world how clever you could be? Get us all running in circles?" He folds the letter and eases it back into its envelope. "Whoever took Saskia did it carefully. There's no sign of struggle at her house, no blood spatter and, so far, no trace of a body."

131

"That's what I'm telling you. She's fine! She's just wandered off."

"She's a mother, Angela. They tend not to do that."

I shrug. "You said people did all kinds of things. You said you'd seen all sorts."

"Somebody's taken her. This is a crime with fore-thought, with intelligent planning."

"It really might not be."

"Freddy Montgomery is a brilliant man with a background in chemical violence and a reputation as being cutthroat when it comes to business."

"Oh, please."

"How else do you think he became a millionaire so fast?"

"His dad gave him a massive leg up. He's got noth-ing to do with Saskia."

"We've asked around. Word on the street is he's meaner than you think. At the very least, I'd say he's an interesting resource."

I feel heat blotch at my neck. "Freddy didn't do any-thing. Just find Saskia already, would you? And leave us all alone."

chapter

12

When I first got home from Oxford a week later, Mom told me my room had been converted into a studio for her music lessons; she was learning to play the harp. All of my possessions were in boxes in the basement.

"Feel free to unpack everything again, darling; it's so lovely to have you back."

I moved into the basement. I piled the boxes of brochures and memorabilia my dad had collected from Boston museums and made myself a bed. I used actual books as a box spring, standing them four-high and eight-abreast at each corner of the tired old mattress with another column in the middle for support. I set out the boundaries of my land in the darkness of that basement, stacking empty wooden wine crates to shoulder height to create a border. I could work on my laptop down there even though the signal was weak. And once I'd fooled them into thinking my marks were good, my parents left me alone, for the most part.

Saskia, on the other hand, was everywhere I went that summer. The first week I got back to Cove, I ended up sitting behind her and HP in the movie theater. (We were a town that only got one movie a month so everyone turned out for it the first Saturday.) They were just three rows ahead of me, sharing a kid-sized popcorn and a bottle of water. All I thought about was how their saliva mixed. She wore a thin leather headband with a small flower at the right temple and her shirt was cut to show the tops of her shoulders. I couldn't tell you anything about the movie.

HP hadn't called me, and once I'd confirmed Saskia was in town, I didn't bother calling him, either. But Cove is so small, it's impossible to avoid conflict for long, and we ran into each other soon enough at the grocery store. He was standing in the dairy aisle, looking at cheese, when I reached for a hacked wedge of Parmesan. He jumped a little when he turned.

"Little John. I had no clue you were back."

Liar.

"Here I am." I dropped the Parmesan into my grocery basket.

"Safe trip over?"

134

I laughed. Obviously it was safe; how else would I be standing in the store? After a pause I spoke carefully. "How's Saskia liking our town?"

He passed a flat packet of cream cheese from one hand to the other as if weighing it, his feet planted square on the fake-wood tiling. The fridges whirred around us and I shivered, hugged my own waist.

"She likes it enough."

"Enough for what? Enough to stay?"

HP cleared his throat. "You look tired. You need more fresh air."

"You know what? You're right. Be sure to come get me when you guys next jog past my house." I walked away from him down the aisle, dropping my basket onto the ground just before I turned the corner.

It was a snippy thing to say, I'll admit, Detective Novak, but it was maddening to see them run together every morning at eight, a pair of happy gazelles bouncing right past my front gate. One morning Mom happened to be coming into the house just as the two of them bounded by. I watched from the door.

"HP?" she said, and he slowed up.

"Oh, hey, Mrs. P." He ran a palm across his forehead. "How's it going?"

"What are you doing? Who's this?" Mom stared right at Saskia, who was jogging on the spot a few paces down, her hands on her hips.

"G'day," Saskia said, and waved. "What a beauty morning, hey?"

"This is my friend Saskia." HP stood tall at the gate in full view from where I was. "She's just visiting."

"It's great here." Saskia beamed. "What a pearler of a town."

"How long is she staying?" Mom put her hand on HP's forearm. "Is everything . . . okay?"

HP looked past her, saw me at the door and shot me a glance.

I said nothing. I just slowly ambled out.

"Oh, Little John, I didn't know you lived here!" Saskia skipped over and rested her elbows on our gate while Mom glared at her. "You's should come out for a run with us! It's a perfect day. You, too, Mrs. . . ." She floundered for a name.

"Petitjean," said my mother. "I don't like to run much. Not publicly."

"Oh, but I know heaps of people your age who get a lot out of a morning run. Are you sure we can't talk you into it?"

If there was a game-show button somewhere that nixed Saskia and slid her into a pit, she'd just pressed it. Even HP flinched.

"People my age?" Mom opened the latch of the gate, forcing Saskia to step back.

"No, I just meant that . . . well, it's like with my mum. She's fifty-one next year and she was finding—"

"Fifty-one?" Mom reeled like she'd just been slapped.

"Come on, Saskia." HP steered her away. "Mrs. Petitjean, we should get going." They walked a few steps before picking up to a jog again.

"Come by for tea!" Mom shouted. She turned and we went inside. "Goodness me."

"I thought you'd like her positive mental approach."

Mom steadied herself against the kitchen counter. "Where in heaven's name did he find her? And why didn't you tell me?"

"He met her at a party."

"Well, he can unmeet her, thank you very much." Mom shuddered. "What is with that accent?"

"She's Australian."

"Well, she can push off back to the outback and leave us all in peace. Are they dating? Angela, tell me they're not dating. Why aren't you more outraged?"

I took a sip of my coffee, enjoying the warmth.

"We could set up a cheese wire from the streetlamp to the porch for when they run back," I suggested. "Take Saskia out at the neck."

"Angela! There's no need to be ridiculous." Then she joined in. "Why don't you spike her Vitamin Water and bundle her onto a plane? Who'd notice a passed-out Australian? All that country does is drink."

I laughed out loud, the first real laugh in a long time. "HP seems to like her," I said.

"Why? She's so . . ." She squared a box in the air with her hands. ". . . symmetrical."

I didn't say anything, but it was the first time in my life I'd ever shared an opinion with my mother. Finally we were starting to align.

Meanwhile, my father was harder to deal with. How many kids do you have, Novak? What, the subject's off-limits? I only bring it up because you don't seem desperate or competitive enough for parenthood. There aren't enough signs that you're living vicariously. The older my father got, the wider and deeper a sense of failure he carried, and the older *I* got the more I realized my purpose in life was to fix it for him. My grades had come in from Oxford substandard and it was all he could talk about all summer. Opportunity wasted this and the trouble I went to that—there wasn't a room I could walk into at home without an ensuing chorus of bleating disappointment.

He even came down to the basement to tell me how inadequate I was. He stood on the other side of my room, tapping his foot on the cement floor while he tried to get a glimpse of me through my wall of wine crates.

"Are you working on fresh college applications?" he called out. "You need to get your transcript in if you have any plans to start your sophomore year."

I turned the page of my Sylvia Plath novel. "I have a college lined up already."

Through the crack I could see him throw his hands to his temples and massage away the day's freshest headache.

"Quit stressing out, Dad. I've got it all taken care of."

"Is it Harvard, Angela? Is it Yale? Is it—oh, I don't know—Stanford?"

He knew exactly who'd offered me a place; it was just that online colleges didn't rate on his academic snob-ometer.

"Let her go where she wants, David," called Mom from the top of the basement stairs. "You're so con-trolling. Isn't he? Why the fixation, David? It's not like you've led the way with a dazzling career path."

Dad rubbed his head harder.

"I'll graduate college. It'll all be fine."

I knew that was like pulling a grenade pin inside his brain, but I didn't care. He followed me to the blackest corners of the house to hint at his intellec-tual frustrations, but he never spelled any of them out exactly, just skirted around their edges. The best way I'd found to deal with my father in battle was to pretend I didn't understand his point.

While he fretted and paced, I'd enrolled in some generic online university—I couldn't care less about which institution I attended: it wasn't like I was going to frame my degree and hang it on the wall. I had a new plan: I wanted to be an archivist, and with the course credits I already had from Oxford, I could take an accelerated program. From one quiet, dank work space to another, and the only company I wanted was books and computers. I'd take literature and library studies and once in the archives of complex systems, I would organize documents into an order that made sense. I'd be doing everyone a favor. Archivists hold history in their hands—they write the endings of all the stories—just think how much everything relies on the input of data these days. The world is littered with unsatisfying closures; it was time somebody took back the helm.

You were angry," Novak cuts in. The sun is setting outside, streaking the table with burnt orange. "You wanted to be in charge because, in reality, you had control over nothing."

"There's something comforting about facts," I concede.

"I like facts, too, Angela." He pats Freddy's letters again, which remain on the table between us. "When

140

people commit their thoughts to paper, it makes things so much easier for us." His eyes burn holes into mine.

"What else have you touched in my room?"

"Oh, we're just getting started."

I shake my head. "Some things are private, you know. Besides, maybe you shouldn't get your finger-prints all over those."

His laugh is measured as he peels his hands from Freddy's top envelope. "What a team player. Don't worry—they already have my prints on file. If this is a *whodunit*"—I can smell the sour coffee on his breath— "I'm pretty sure they know it wasn't me."

I didn't escape seeing Saskia a few more times through that summer. I waited in line behind her at the grocery store, listening to her brag to the sad-eyed cashier about the year she'd just spent in Europe. *It was bloody awesome*, she said before she caught sight of me. *Oh, Little John, good on ya! Wasn't Oxford so beaut? You were there—you know.* In July she pulled over in HP's truck to offer me a ride when she saw me walking along the street alone. I had headphones in and didn't acknowledge she'd stopped. And then, maybe a week later, she made a point of veering towards me at the movie theater when I was standing in the doorway looking at the posters.

"Are you watching this one, LJ? You can sit with

us." She was holding hands with HP as she said it, even though it looked like he was trying to let go.

"I'm not . . . I'm just looking."

"Sure, darl? The offer's there."

She was like a child, wandering out of a burning building, with no concept whatsoever that she'd lit the match.

Mom hovered two steps behind me most of the summer. One evening as I sat quietly on the porch, she came out of the house holding an empty mason jar. She'd labeled it, and the lid was open.

"Darling." She patted my knee, but her nails dented my flesh. "I've been having a think. I've found this jar and according to research, whatever you put in here comes true." Her eyes were watery.

"What research?" I took the jar and rotated it slowly. Across the label she'd written MANIFESTATIONS in swirly cursive.

"Well, the girls at my music class if I'm honest, but darling, I've looked it up on the World Wide Web and all of it's true. You take little pieces of paper, write down your hopes and dreams and pop them into the jar."

I put both fists to my chin, leaning on my knees.

"Whatever you put out into the universe is an

energy that changes everything." Her voice rose like an evangelist on TV. "It's manifest destiny."

I snorted.

"It can't hurt to try, can it? I mean"—she took the jar back and hugged it to her chest—"we've all had a miserable summer. But it's time to forgive and forget—you know?—and get life back on track now. Isn't it, my beautiful girl? Come on, look alive." She slapped my knee with a rousing palm. "You have so much going for you, and nobody likes a Droopy Drawers."

I kept the jar for a couple of weeks, scribbling all of my nineteen-year-old angst onto paper scraps and dropping them into the glass, the thickness of which only magnified my vitriol when held up to the light. After that, I threw the jar out in the trash. Nothing was coming true. At least, that's what I thought then; but here, now, it's frightening to think that maybe Mom's witchy voodoo might have worked, albeit more slowly than she thought. Saskia's vanished, hasn't she? It's kind of terrible, although deep down, in a part of me I'll never let anyone see, I also don't mind if she doesn't come back. That sounds bad, I know. But people can't always control their thoughts; they just control what they do about them. Saskia came in like a hurricane that summer, ripping whole dwellings apart, and maybe Mom was right. The energy you put out into the world does change everything.

About a month later, in September, HP left a voice mail on my cell, the first message I'd received from him since getting back from Oxford.

"There's a party at Fu Bar tonight." He'd called at 5:30 p.m. Thanks for the afterthought. "Everyone will be there. Saskia's visa ran out so it's a good-bye thing. Later." His tone was curt.

"God bless the department of immigration," said Mom when I told her.

"I don't know why he thinks I'd show up to her good-bye party." I picked at the label of a bottle of beer I'd opened. Mom eyed me, hoping I'd fetch a glass.

"But you must go. Darling, it'd be good for you. Go out for the evening, kick up your heels. You've been holed up here in this cave for months; it's not good to spend so much time alone. Come, I'll help you pick out an outfit."

"Nothing fits."

"Well, you're thin right now. You need to eat a bit more." She tried to tuck my hair behind my ear, but I pulled away. "You look striking with those high cheekbones of yours. And now HP is going to be on his own . . ."

"I guess Ezra will be there. I could just talk to him all night."

"That'd be all right, wouldn't it?" Her forehead creased and her smile seemed quivery. I let her pick out clothes for me while I sat on my makeshift bed sipping a beer. She pulled out black leggings and a striped black top from the piles on the basement floor. The top hung loose off one shoulder.

"Beautiful as ever," Mom said once I put them on. "Now let's find you some footwear."

Fu Bar hadn't changed, apart from the installation of a stereo system that now made it impossible to hear what anyone was ordering. I was late getting there and the place was packed, mostly with faces I recognized from grades below me. As I grabbed a beer, I spotted HP, Saskia and Ezra at a circle booth in the back and wove through the crowd towards them. HP wore a tank top, his shoulders freckled and dark. Between him and Ezra sat Saskia, smiling, all of her teeth shining too brightly. Every now and then, she sipped at a clear liquid in a tall glass.

Ezra spied me and waved as I approached. "Little John! Get over here, stranger." He bumped the other two along the curved bench to make room for me beside him. I squeezed in. From my seat, I could see Saskia's hand on HP's thigh.

"It's good you came," HP shouted over the music. "I'll be right back."

147

I watched him move through the throng, laughing with people, slapping them on the back. After a second or two, I slid out of the booth and headed through the swinging doors to the washroom corridor. I sipped my beer and waited.

He walked out of the men's room wiping his hands on the back pockets of his jeans. "Hey." He stopped short of the door. "You waiting for me?"

"I just need to say that I never slept with anybody in the world but you, I never wanted to, I never even kissed . . ." He put up his hand to stop me and I petered out. We stood there, both of us with our arms crossed. In the end he leaned his back against the wall and we stayed there like that, watching people come and go from the bathrooms.

"Listen, I asked you to come because I hope we can end this Cold War." I frowned and he added, "Yes, I know you're not Russian. I'm being what-do-you-call-it."

"Figurative."

"I've missed you, LJ."

"Bullshit."

He sighed. "Are you leaving town? For college?"

"Nope. Studying online."

"I got a permanent job coaching at the high school. Like, year-round. It's pretty sick. I start in a week or so." His jaw muscle clenched and unclenched. "I'm dropping the carpentry but my dad says I can pick up my apprenticeship whenever I want."

"That's good."

"What were you doing with Freddy that night in Oxford?"

I think of the tepid champagne on the stone balcony, the wriggly pudginess of Freddy's hips. "Nothing."

"Okay." He exhaled, like the whole muddle could finally be over.

"Is Saskia leaving forever?" The last word rose into a squeak.

"I guess." He looked down at his feet. "Why don't you like her?"

"HP, she's so . . . vanilla."

"What's that supposed to mean?"

Ezra's head appeared through the doorway. "We're saying good-bye." He glanced quickly from my face to HP's. "You should come out here, bro."

HP frowned like he wanted to say more to me, but instead we pushed through the doors to hear Saskia's tinny accent. "I've made so many friends, you's all have been heaps kind."

She said it like this—*koind*. The people around her had hoisted her up to her feet; she stood on the bench cushion with her bony knees poking out of beach-bleached shorts. Her blue-elephant tattoo shimmered.

"I wish I could take you fellas back with me to

'Straya." The first syllable of her country had vanished and the last one bounced. The pod of leering guys in the booth cheered and raised their beer bottles. "Look, I want to say a special thank-you to Hamish . . ."

Everyone looked around, confused.

"To *HP* . . ." More cheers. "For putting me up all summer! Here's to you, Haym."

I thought I might vomit into the neck of my beer bottle. To my left, HP raised his hand and blushed.

"And while I'm up here, I just wanted to give you this." She arched forwards towards HP, an envelope in her outstretched hand. Someone took it and started passing it back to HP. "Fair dinkum. See what you think."

While he opened the envelope, Saskia did this strange little curtsy of excitement. He pulled out an airline ticket, Qantas, the rigid white of it stark in the air.

"Jesus, Sask." HP scratched his head. "How'd you . . ."

"Call it an investment," she said, and she winked at me. At *me*.

The room erupted into whoops and hollers, with all the boys shaking HP at the shoulder like he'd just won a competition. He stood there staring at Saskia, who remained marooned in the booth. She battled her way over the back of the bench towards him.

"There goes your job at the high school," I said to HP as Saskia arrived beside us.

"Look, you don't have to use the ticket now . . . or at all. I can get a refund." Her eyelashes looked longer with her head lowered.

"No, it's super generous and nice of you, Sask, it's just, I—"

"HP has a life here," I said. "He's—"

HP interrupted. "Actually, it's just I never thought I'd travel. I'd always kind of ruled it out."

Apparently, England didn't count.

He looked at Saskia, his face open and shocked. She beamed at him. I stood watching them, feeling loss creep over me, slick like oil.

I didn't say good-bye to anybody that night, although Saskia stopped me at the door—she must have been tracking my exit.

"I hope we can be friends." Her entire face lit up like the sun.

I looked straight into her eyes. "Why don't you ever say what you mean?"

She'd been sipping through her straw and coughed a little. There was a rearranging of goodwill features. "Angela. For starters, I'm not trying to—"

"You bought him a flight to Sydney!" My mouth felt flinty, like granite.

"He's coming back, but . . ." The possibility hung pointlessly at the end of her sentence.

"But not without you," I said.

"Haym really cares about you." There was such an earnest arc to her eyebrows. It made me want to set them on fire.

"It's a problem, isn't it? Don't worry; there'll be plenty of time and space on the other side of the planet for you to reshape him."

I walked away from her, straight home, without turning back once to see the look on her face.

Novak rubs his hands together. "It can't have been easy."

"Which part?"

"Competing with an all-expenses-paid trip to a different hemisphere. I can see why you don't like her."

"I don't compete with her. She's dull and predictable."

He scratches his jaw. "So when did HP head down under?"

"The next month. It was kind of a flurry. I didn't even see him again before he left."

"Did you hear from him after? Was he as good a pen pal as Freddy?"

He's being ironic. Novak thinks he's driving this story. He thinks he's ten steps ahead of me.

"We Skyped a couple of times, but Saskia was always right there in the background, butting in. They stayed at her parents' place in Manly Beach and from what I could tell did nothing but surf and watch sunrises. I stalked her on Facebook. She wrote poems about water and light and posted them on her wall. Her security settings are child-like."

"How long did HP stay over there?"

I pause. This is just pretense. Novak flicks through his file with his head down.

"Oh, here it is. Yes, okay, okay. So." He looks up. "Did HP call you about his plans to wed?"

The mention of it still makes my mouth turn sour, yet Novak's build to this moment is nothing less than thespian genius. I have to give him credit for that: my mother would be proud of him. What he already knows is that HP wrote me early in the new year, a few months after he landed in Sydney. Novak knows this because he would have found the letter by now, which I have always kept in its airmail envelope against the mirror on my dresser, every line of which is also seared into my brain. It wasn't a well-written letter, mostly about the flora and fauna of Australia, as if HP was dreading writing the final paragraph.

Things have happened and plans have changed, he wrote in scrawly slanted lettering that looked like it was trying to dig its heels in on the page. *Life throws*

*curveballs and the best you can do is swing at them.
Who knows? Maybe I'll hit this one out of the park. I've
asked Sask to be my wife. I don't think she saw it coming,
but she's excited. We'll have a ceremony on the beach,
nothing too flash, you know me. Sask has a dress but
she won't let me see it—says it's bad luck. Her mom's telling everyone we've set a date and there's a buzz around
town, people keep shaking my hand. I hope you're okay.
I miss you. Everything's changing but not that.*

A month later he and Saskia were married.

Novak tosses a curly-edged photograph onto the
table. HP and Saskia sitting on surfboards, the ocean
shapeless behind them. They're wearing leis and above
their heads on fingers clasped together is the new glint
of wedding rings.

"I've seen that photo before."

"You didn't attend the wedding?"

"I wasn't invited. Nobody was. It was in fucking
Sydney."

"Ezra wasn't best man?"

"Saskia's brother. He was, like, twelve."

Novak rests his hands in his lap. "Would you have
gone if you had been invited? Would you have looked
happy in the photographs?"

He's definitely getting to know me.

"Did you get them a gift at least?"

"I framed a photo of HP, me and Ezra from grad

and sent it in the mail. It cost me a lot to send. I never heard if it got to them."

"They decided to move back here and had a party in Cove when they returned." It's not a question. Novak's putting it all together for me. How kind. "You went to the party with your old pal Freddy Montgomery. And this was . . ." He's flipping pages again. ". . . six years ago?"

I chew my thumbnail, hoping he won't ask me the next question, but it's inevitable. "So at the party when they moved back, she must have been—"

"Pregnant."

"With their daughter." He looks up. "With HP's child."

It's the detail he's been waiting for, and he watches my face. Every muscle in my being tightens so that no emotion escapes me.

SATURDAY

chapter

14

It's dark outside now. Once in a while, the sweep of a car's headlights crosses the far wall as new visitors pull into the police station parking lot. The clock hand jars past twelve.

Novak's been gone for hours. He just up and left with Freddy's private letters. For a guy who's got me for only a limited time, he's letting a lot of the night slip away. At around ten, a policeman with thick ears and a ruddy face brought me a plate of macaroni, which he deposited wordlessly onto the table, clattering me a fork. The macaroni had congealed on the plate. I didn't touch it.

I'm desperate to sleep, but there's nowhere to lie down. Once in a while, I rest the side of my head on the table, the cool surface smooth against my ear; but my lower back curves awkwardly and soon enough I have to sit up again.

Has the whole department gathered by the coffee machine to talk about me? If I stay here much longer I'll need a lawyer, because Novak is missing the point. If he spent more time actually listening, he'd be able to see the truth. Everything would become clear. It wouldn't hurt, either, if he tried to be a little nicer. The only gesture of kindness was that cup of coffee and that never turned out to be real.

When HP left me and shacked up with Saskia, I lost any feeling of safety. Without him next to me, reality stopped being manageable: my brain wouldn't flex anymore. HP took his happiness and spent it elsewhere, blanketed other people in it, while here I've been miserable for six years straight, not that anyone's noticed. It's a longer sentence than some people serve in jail. By day, it's the boredom that gets me. Most people seem able to pad themselves with things they hope to learn or buy or achieve, but everything they're aiming at is dull. Why bother to pretend that life's not ultimately unsatisfying?

I read once that in a game of cat and mouse, the only way for the mouse to win is to walk willingly into the cat's mouth. I think about that a lot. Futility's staring directly at us. We should just stop running.

The truth is, I didn't know Saskia was pregnant when I showed up to that garden party. When I told my mom they were having a wedding celebration, she closed her eyes and kept them shut for the best part of a minute. She was drinking coffee at the time, the steam from the cup curling around her chin. When she finally opened her eyes, they glistened with tears.

"I can't believe he's going through with it. Are *you* all right, darling? Why on earth are you going to their party?"

"Just to see HP."

"That poor lost boy. Well, don't engage with the Australian. Petitjean women do not allow others the opportunity to gloat."

By the kitchen cupboard, Dad let out a wheeze of air that sounded like sarcasm. He was stirring sugar into a cup of tea.

"Is there something I can help you with, David?" My mother's fingers gripped her coffee mug so hard that her fingertips pressed white near the rim. "Or did you have something to add?"

"Come on, Shelley. Can't people marry who they want to marry?"

"Yes, but sometimes they regret their decision later," Mom snapped back.

Dad paused by the back of the sofa before shuffling to his study, where he quietly shut the door.

Ezra was absent also—he was trying out for a pro water polo team in North Carolina and I always thought the fact HP didn't reschedule the party to accommodate Ez was surefire proof that the event was more Saskia's than his. In the same vein, HP's parents hosted the party in their front yard but you could tell it was Saskia's planning because it was all fairy lights and butterfly-themed cupcakes. They'd even hired a string quartet to play theme tunes from Disney movies, for God's sake.

Yes, I went to the party with Freddy Montgomery. While HP had been doing his sun salutations in Sydney, the one positive development in my life had been Freddy moving to New York City. At least one weekend out of every four, he came to visit me. I was lonely in Cove: I started my online degree but didn't have anyone to hang out with. Ezra was around, but he was either working weird shifts at the grocery store or training for his one shot at being a pro athlete. I welcomed the attention of Freddy. He showered me with gifts and I accepted them. Maybe I shouldn't have, but it wasn't like anybody else's spotlight was on me.

When we walked into the garden party, I realized I hadn't set foot on their property since before I left for Oxford, but the old birch tree was still there, stalwart and notched with secrets. It seemed a lifetime ago that HP and I had huddled against the bark.

Freddy headed straight to the drinks table, which was Old Man Parker's workbench set up to the right of the house with an embroidered sheet thrown across it. Freddy hesitated, his Rolex glinting on his outstretched wrist. Novak's right about Freddy's fast fortune: whether or not his rise had been Machiavellian, money sat on every part of him now; it seeped from his very skin. He was more groomed than he'd been at Oxford, more spa-treated and fine-tailored. That day he was dressed in a pale-gray suit with a pink collared shirt while everyone else wore ball caps and shorts. At the drinks table, Freddy turned to show me a silver angel that hooked and tinkled at the base of each wineglass's stem.

"What a glorious touch," he said, meaning the opposite. "Where on earth have you brought me, Ms. Petitjean? The style palette's verging on Ikea."

We hardly mingled. Freddy and I hung back by the tree, while Freddy pointed out all the ways in which party guests were wearing their clothes wrongly. *Look at that tapered waist! Go up a size, love. There's no shame in it.*

It was harmless enough, as afternoons go, until I returned from the bathroom inside the house to find that Saskia had discovered Freddy. He stood with one arm across his waist and the other one dangling a half-filled wineglass, which moved in rhythm with plot points of his anecdote. Saskia's dress was a deep threat of red, and while Freddy told his story she gaped at him, the fingertips of her right hand on the upper arm of his suit sleeve.

"You're funny as!" She giggled, with that way she had of ruining the simile. "Come and meet my new rellies!"

She dragged him over to HP's mom and dad, both of whom stood quietly throughout the party holding hands. Mrs. Parker had on a dress, but nothing else about her shouted grand celebration. Were they surprised by the turn of events? I hadn't had a chance to ask them. I dawdled a few steps behind, mainly because without Freddy alongside me, the whole afternoon took on a more difficult complexity.

"Parko," trilled Saskia to one or both of HP's parents, "this is Freddy Montgomery."

"How do you do? What a pleasure it is." Freddy bowed slightly to HP's mother, who caught my eye as I stood a foot behind. "You must be terribly proud of your son."

Was Freddy being ironic? He'd yet to glance back at me.

"We are, we are. Especially proud what with their news."

Mrs. Parker looked straight at me. She always had such gentle eyes, and at that moment, I saw her flinch.

"News?" Freddy asked, as though he didn't know. Saskia put a delicate hand to her belly. *Shhhh*, she mimed, with one straight finger against her lips. She took a breath to launch into her life's most recent elation, but I backed away towards the house again, through the kitchen and into the cool leather of the armchair in the shadiest corner of the Parkers' screened-in sunroom.

Mrs. Parker had been knitting a sweater—it lay wrapped in a wicker basket at the base of the chair, ready to be woven on like a story. I held up the wool, wondering who it was for, just as Freddy wandered into the room.

"How are you holding up?" He flopped down onto the sofa, which was less spongy than he'd anticipated. His wine spilled and he smudged it into the fabric of the cushion.

I didn't feel like responding. Freddy lounged across the sunroom from me, staring at the general layout.

"Do you think he married her because she's pregnant?"

"Would there be any other reason?" He reached over and got rid of the wineglass, depositing it on a tall-legged coffee table. "I mean, aside from the years he can look forward to jogging or eating kale?"

"Do you think he loves her?"

"No. I think he loves you and got her."

I plucked at the stitching in the upholstery. "You talk like it's food in a diner. But if the order's wrong, why wouldn't he send it back?"

"Because some men are like that: they have to taste what's in front of them, and before they know it they've eaten too much and have to pay for it." Freddy sniffed the fabric of the sofa. "My jacket is going to need a dry clean. Are there cats in this house?" He clicked his fingers a few times, demanding my focus. "Angela, I want you to know that I would never get the order wrong in the diner. The obvious truth here, my darling, is that you are not diner fare." He waited.

"Let's get out of here." I pushed myself up from the chair. "This whole town, I mean."

"That's the spirit." We left the sunroom and when we moved through the kitchen, HP was there. Freddy walked straight past him into the living room. HP and I were alone.

"Little John." HP took two big steps towards me, playing with the gold ring on his hand. "Listen, I'm sorry I didn't get a chance to speak with you much while I was over in Oz . . . it kind of got . . . it's been crazy hectic lately, I kind of feel like my head is spinning."

"Wait till the baby's on the outside. I hear that gets busy."

He blinked. "It's not a shotgun wedding, you know."

166

"Okay."

"She's only a little more than a month along. And I didn't think we were telling people." His collar looked tight as he reefed at it. "It wasn't planned, sure, but maybe it's just about, you know, getting to a place faster than you'd meant to."

He was babbling.

"You play the cards you're dealt. Everyone does." His voice was rising.

"I thought there was always a chance to get a new hand," I said.

His shoulders slumped. "I'm sorry, LJ. Fuck, I know I've hurt you. I know that's why you're . . . being like this." His eyes were deep and dark like nighttime. Like the skies we used to sleep under in the bed of his truck. "But honestly, my heart broke, too, somewhere along the way."

I felt my ribs contract. If I moved too quickly, I knew I'd sob. Meanwhile, HP looked like he was going to reach out and hug me.

"I didn't even think we were done, and then you're suddenly overseas, and then getting married. And now . . . this. It's just . . . a lot to take in." We weren't touching but in the gap between us, a hum of connection surged. I was sure he felt it, too.

"Not to say anything bad about Saskia. I'm not— you know—speaking badly of her." He sighed. "But

167

you and me—if this had all been the other way around and you'd done this to me, I know for sure I'd have kicked that guy's ass."

"Who's to say I won't kick hers?"

We laughed, oh *ha ha ha*.

"It's good to talk to you, LJ. I want us to be in each other's lives. We grew up together—it means something. And you're my first love. That's forever. That's set in stone."

I looked down at the floor tiles. "You know, I don't want you to call me LJ anymore, or Little John. I'm going with Angela from now on."

"Really?" He frowned. "I don't think Angela's you."

The front door swung open and Mrs. Parker walked into the house carrying two halves of a broken wineglass. Her index finger dripped blood.

HP sprang forwards and grabbed some paper towels from the roll on the counter.

"So silly," Mrs. Parker said, her head fluttering. "I was just picking up the pieces and one of them sliced me." HP pressed the towel to her finger and guided her to the sink. "How are you?"

It took me a second to understand she was speaking to me.

"Oh, okay." I cleared my throat. "It's a nice party."

Mrs. Parker glanced at me, with meaning. "Well done for coming."

"I was just leaving, actually. But thank you. It's always good to see you, Mrs. Parker."

She wrapped the towel around her finger and kissed her son's cheek, then touched my face softly as well with her one good hand. "I'll leave you to your chat."

The kitchen felt awkward once she'd left. Neither HP nor I could make eye contact.

"I should go," I said.

HP turned and swept me into a hug with such force that it lifted me onto my tiptoes. His entire frame held me up, braced me: if I'd relaxed every muscle in my body, I wouldn't have slumped an inch.

And that's what Novak's not getting, what he doesn't see. It's not about the drinks HP didn't buy me or the hours he spent on his own. It's about who your soul mate is. Ask HP's mom. Even she knows. Guys like HP hug like that to tell you something. Something that means forever.

chapter

15

Novak's returned with renewed vigor, as if he spent the hour between twelve and one downing cans of Red Bull. I wish he'd brought me the coffee he'd promised. With the exception of two bathroom breaks, I've been sitting in this room for almost sixteen hours now. I'm starting to see double.

"We've just confirmed: Saskia Parker's DNA is all over that elephant necklace."

"Is that what you've been doing all this time?" I close my eyes. "I thought you already knew it was her necklace—you have it in a bag with her name on the label."

Novak balks. He looks like a kid who's presented his best artwork and been told it's not that special. He stands, pacing to the window. Outside, the sky has been engulfed by darkness.

"Believe me, we're getting somewhere. Fast. You should, too."

"Right. Sure, Novak. Let me get on that."

He sweeps his hair to the side and stares out the window.

"Who else's DNA is on the necklace?" I ask.

"Why aren't you asking where we found it?"

"Well, wherever it was, I didn't put it there."

He watches me for a moment. "We're looking into Freddy. You know that, right? Tell me what you know. What's relevant, I mean."

It's absurd how lost Novak is. He's seriously their homicide guy? I could find Saskia quicker myself.

"Isn't Freddy in one of your rooms down the corridor? Anything you want to know, you could probably ask him yourself."

He continues staring out the window. "What was his apartment like? You spent a lot of time there."

"You're asking the wrong questions. You already have all your answers."

"I have some of them." He turns his head slightly. "How much time did you spend with him in his New York apartment?"

With his back to me, the line of skin below Novak's

hairline is startlingly white, as if it's never before been exposed to sunlight.

"Are you asking about Freddy because you think he's madly in love with me? That he'd do anything I asked of him? My God, this is ridiculous."

"Is it? What *would* he do for you? How far would he go?"

"You'd have to ask him."

"Am I right that Freddy shares your contempt for Saskia?"

"I'd say he's sympathetic."

Novak slopes against the wall with his hands in his pants pockets. He looks like a menswear ad, the kind my dad would respond to. "Why didn't you move in with him?"

"Because I wasn't in love with him."

"Who were you in love with?"

Novak wants my answer to be HP. He's literally bending at the knee, waiting to pounce on it.

"I stayed in Cove, if that's what you're asking, because it gets comfortable living where you've grown up. You know? We're all creatures of habit."

Novak laughs quietly.

"My dad bought a little house by the lake so I moved into it. It was easier to stay than go."

"Didn't HP and Saskia live in a house by the lake?"

"It's a big lake." We stare at each other, but his eyes are colder than mine. "Mom came to visit me a lot. She liked Freddy even more than I did: he was rich, successful—"

"Wait, what?" Novak pushes forwards and hurries to his chair. "Your mother had a connection with Freddy?"

There you go, Novak. You're welcome. "I'm not sure if you'd call it a connection. I mean, if you ask me, it was a little one-sided. Mom liked that Freddy was articulate and refined. *He's debonair like a young Laurence Olivier, darling, or a Ralph Fiennes.*"

He's really scribbling now.

"So, did she make actual advances on him?"

"Advances?" I take pleasure in saying it: "Oh, I suppose. I couldn't say for sure how Freddy responded to them. Sometimes guys say one thing and do another. Don't you find?"

Novak spins in his chair and signals to the camera in the far corner. It's a circular motion with his right hand, as if he's twirling a tiny hoop on his forefinger. *Run the tape? Check the facts? Go get Shelley Petitjean?* It's a call to action, that much is clear.

"What did your mother say when she heard Saskia was pregnant with HP's child?"

"Nothing. She covered her face with her hands."

Suddenly Novak smacks the table, making me

jump. "Where's Saskia? Who's got her? Is it Freddy? Or your mom? Are we really going to have to do this the hard way?" He crouches to get a proper view of my face. "Is Saskia dead, Angela? Is she being held? Or worse? If you know anything—anything at all—do you understand what it means not to tell me?" His next question comes out as a roar. "*Why don't you care?*"

I slide my hands under my thighs. Novak sits down, knocking his chair back a few inches, and when I glance up he's smoothing his hair back into place.

"Do you know where we found Saskia's elephant necklace, Angela?"

"I've told you, no."

"In your copy of *Jane Eyre*. On your bedside table. *That* is what we need to talk about."

chapter

16

The necklace was put into my book. She did it secretly. I swear I had no clue it was in there until Novak yelled the fact at me. It must have been pressed in a curl between pages near the back, the weight of the book holding it fast. Novak doesn't believe me, of course. He won't consider that someone *else* put it there. No, he's convinced I'm the villain, even though one necklace can't prove anything. He's biding his time, one eye on the clock, one hand on his pager, hoping somebody will bring him something conclusive. In the meantime, he badgers me with endless questions. *Why did you stay so close to the Parkers? Weren't you just torturing yourself?* His desperation to be done with me is sketched thick around him like a caricature. The interview's draining us both: I'm

177

as fidgety as he is. But we're locked in now, two tired swimmers clinging to the same rope, neither of us able to let go until we reach the safety of an ending.

Why *did* I stay in Cove? It's a good question, but at the time I just remember thinking that I needed to be around the familiar. And where else was I meant to go? HP was here. But as much as I wanted to run into him, our meetings were frustratingly rare. I suppose our schedules didn't match any longer—once I was done with my degree, I worked every day until past four, and he was coaching full-time at Lakeside High—they'd delayed hiring him until he got back from Australia. I'm not sure what he did when he clocked off at 3 p.m., but most likely he went home to renovate his house. He built a home while Saskia built a baby. She wasn't the only one doing that: quite a few girls I'd graduated with were now pushing strollers around the grocery store, looking shadowy-eyed and bewildered. The rest of my grad class had fled the town—only the marrying kind remained. Beyond that, a new wave of eighteen-year-olds swaggered around like they owned the place. They had no idea how much harder life would get for them.

Unlike HP, Saskia was easier to find. In the months after their wedding celebration she grew more and more swollen. By Halloween, when we crossed paths in the furniture store, she must have been eight months pregnant. She looked like the pumpkins on our porch.

"We hadn't planned to start a family so soon," she crooned, caressing the curve of her belly under her stretched-out Billabong fleece. "But you know, with HP, it's hard to turn the guy down!"

I smiled with the lower half of my face. Mom was with me, shopping for new bedding for the lakeside house. At the time, I hadn't realized it would be her who would sleep in it.

"You move fast," I heard Mom say behind me. "Is that an Australian thing?"

"Pardon?" Saskia pronounced the word as if it contained four *a*'s.

"You know, early Australians battling through the mangroves, fighting back malaria, all convicts together building a home?"

Saskia brushed long bangs from her forehead, watching Mom test the thread count of cotton sheets by rolling them between her thumb and forefinger.

"Are you having a boy or a girl?" My tone was flat.

"Hopefully one or the other," she trilled.

Nobody laughed.

Mom touched my shoulder lightly. "I'm sure it'll be a little angel, whatever it is."

"Thanks, that's nice." Saskia turned to me. "LJ, we

should rent a movie together and eat popcorn in our tracky dacks. Girls' night. It would be heaps fun."

She hugged me good-bye and left us to wander on through the store. Mom turned to me.

"I can't stand her."

I didn't say a word.

A week before the baby was born, HP called me from school and asked if we could meet up for a drink.

"What, in the evening time?" I asked. I was totally taken aback.

"Early evening for an hour or so? It's nothing major; I just want to see you."

I tried not to sound too excited. "Um, Friday's free for me."

"Perfect. Four o'clock at Fu?"

"Sure."

It was the start of December and snowing for the first time. When I walked over to the bar, the flakes were fluffy and lovable in ways they would no longer be come February. There wasn't much traffic, and everything felt still, quiet. Fairy lights twinkled in the apartment buildings above the shops on Main Street, and in some windows I could just make out the side of a Christmas tree. People were buying them earlier and earlier: soon stores would sell them as a two-for-one deal with Thanksgiving turkeys.

At Fu Bar things had changed. Tinkering jazz

played on the stereo, a light flutter of piano keys here, a soft saxophone there. The bar was empty, aside from a few murmuring lawyer types on barstools, drinking European beer in tall glasses and shaking salted almonds in their fists like dice before dropping them into their mouths.

I took a seat at a table far enough from the door. HP came in at ten past four. He wore a black bomber jacket and trendy, dark jeans that Saskia must have had a say in. His dockworker-style toque was pocked with snow; he took it off and banged it against his thigh.

"Am I late?" He checked an oversized watch at his wrist that looked like it would save him in a survival situation. "Sorry, the roads are ugly coming in from the lake." He settled into his chair, his cheeks flushed with cold. "Have you been here awhile?"

"No." I looked around. "Look at this place. Nothing's the same."

"You should see it out back. The Ping-Pong tables are gone and the back deck's now a terraced barbecue area . . ." He faltered as he mentioned the area we'd kissed in two short years ago. "Anyway, you look lovely. Elegant." He stared at me in my thin black sweater.

"Thank you."

"How's life? Are you still working at the library?"

"No, I got a new position in vital statistics. It pays more and it's more . . . interesting."

181

"Well, good, that's good. You need to be challenged." He'd learned teacher-speak. Had he invited me here for career guidance? "How are things with your folks?"

"Oh, they're all right, I guess. They fight a lot. You know how they are. Anyway, I'm less idealistic these days about true love and partnership."

HP flinched just a little.

"Fifty percent of marriages end in divorce," I said. "Imagine if the odds were the same with skydiving. Would you really jump?"

"Ha," he responded, and squirmed in his seat. The bartender—a man in his early thirties with a Merlot-colored apron tied around the waist of his jeans—arrived at the side of our table.

"Is this a coffee thing, or . . . ?"

"I'll have a glass of the house red. It's that kind of weather," I said.

The bartender nodded.

"I'll take a whiskey. Single shot, single malt, on ice."

HP waited a second or two. "So . . . are you dating?"

"A little bit." I wasn't.

"Guys from around Cove?"

"Maybe." I played with the delicate silver charm at my neck.

"Okay, well, look, I just wanted to meet up with you before—" The barman arrived with our drinks.

HP waited until he'd gone again. "Before the baby's born."

"It must be any day." My wine lilted thick and bloodred as I lifted the curve of the glass into my palm. "I saw Saskia about a month ago and she looked ready to pop."

"Yeah, she's almost ready. We're gearing up here."

"I feel like everyone's getting busier and busier."

HP eyed me as I spoke, rocking his glass from side to side so that the ice cubes bumped. "Totally. Mortgages and taxes. Who saw that coming? The last time I checked, we were hanging out at the Tarzan swing and our only worry was avoiding a sunburn."

"Where's Ezra?" I asked. "He's vanished." Which wasn't true—I'd seen him at the grocery store several times. He didn't like Saskia and told me every time I saw him. Said she was a drill sergeant cleverly disguised. *She's changed him, LJ. She's ironed him straight.*

"Ezra hasn't vanished," HP said. "You have."

"Oh." I sipped more wine. "Have I?"

"I never see you."

"How hard are you trying?" *Be nice, Angela. Be nice or he'll leave.* "I haven't vanished, HP. At least not from you."

He rolled the base of his glass around his coaster in an orbit. "We worry about you, you know. Don't disappear on me, okay?"

"Listen," I began, pausing to wonder whether I was brave enough for this sentence, "it's not easy. I get that you're married and all that, but for me . . ." I took a deep breath. ". . . for me it's complicated. I've got left-overs."

HP frowned.

"Feelings that don't fit anywhere anymore."

"Oh, I see." He looked down at his glass.

"Don't you?"

"Umm," he floundered. He didn't say no.

"That's not to say I don't want to be in your life," I clarified.

"No, good." HP scratched his head. "Because that's what I'd really like. It would be nice if I could count on you. And Saskia thinks it's important, too."

Bullshit.

"We can be friends, can't we?" He reached his hand across the table. I took it. His skin was as warm and smooth as I remembered but his fingers had thick-ened, probably from all the carpentry and housework. Still, I didn't want to let go.

"Somebody's got to tell my kid how cool I was in high school. Ezra will never admit it." His eyes were soft and glassy. It was my touch. I was sure of it.

"We can be friends," I said, still holding his hand, pushing my electricity through it. "That's how it all began, right?"

"Right." He pulled away, sat back, relieved, and then checked his watch. For a moment I imagined myself ripping it from his wrist and throwing it across the room.

"I've got to say, I don't think I can tell your kid you were cool in high school. You know me." I looked down at my wine. "I never was a very good liar."

Novak probably thinks I'm a masochist, but that's simply not true. Things changed when Olive was born. No, I didn't visit HP and Saskia in the hospital, but I did take flowers over to their house once they were home with the baby. Carnations.

HP had been working on a fixer-upper down by the lake—a ramshackle old place with a wraparound porch. He'd already rebuilt the entire bottom floor. It smelled of sawdust and fresh paint. Olive slept the whole time I was there. She was painfully beautiful, her little fists clenched as she took milky, fast breaths. Blond, velveteen hair swept circular in a helix from the crown of her head.

"You want to hold her?" HP wore his old track T-shirt from high school, and his face was puffy with sleeplessness. It was two weeks since we'd sat in the bar together.

"Let's leave her," Saskia urged. She was already back in her skinny jeans. She craned in past my shoulder to peep into the crib and I could smell her—her faint, frangipani-petal sweetness. The three of us stood together, a line of faces, a little team of awe. I stepped back and away.

"It's really nice of you to come over," HP said. "You look well."

"Appearances are deceptive."

"You're not well?"

"No, no. Just kidding. I'm fine."

"Well, you should come visit us more, Little John."

"You can't call her Little John anymore. She's Angela," Saskia said. "*Angela*, it's such a pretty name."

"It's true," HP said. He put his hand on my shoulder but he was looking at his wife. "Listen, Saskia and I have been thinking, and we'd like to ask if you'd be Olive's godmother."

I tried not to look horrified.

"Uh, gosh," I said. *Godmother?*

"Is that a yes?" Saskia was beaming at me.

"Of course!" Laughter, smiles and hugs, smiles and hugs.

I wondered why they welcomed me into their life with this invitation, but when I told Mom about it, she was uncharacteristically positive.

"You should take that opportunity and run with it, darling," she said, sorting her clothes on the bed into piles of keep and giveaway. The giveaway pile was huge. "As much as we don't like the show, we might as well get you a leading role in it."

So as it turned out, I got over myself and accepted the chance to be a part of the Parkers' lives. I started to spend more and more time at HP and Saskia's house, and began to actually feel useful.

"I told you we needed your help," HP said one day while I was holding Olive. "Your mom's pleased, too. It's a win–win."

I wasn't sure what my mother had contributed to the situation, but having Olive around me all the time was like a joint I didn't know I had, clicking smoothly into socket. It was a physical improvement: being near the baby as she cooed and discovered her toes meant that any blocked frustrations in me started to turn fluid and change color. A few months into being her godmother, what poured out of me into Olive was pure connection, a gentle force. I was almost a third parent.

Like my mom had predicted, it was good to be a strong influence in Olive's life, and as she grew up I grew closer and closer to her. I never missed a birthday, and every year I bought her a chocolate cupcake, replacing the fondant butterfly with a Lego Star Wars figurine. Saskia asked me not to buy the ones with the little, detachable helmets—choking hazard—but seriously, our parents never worried about stuff like that and we all made it.

Olive's eyes were a deep, inky indigo, a feline curve to the edges. She was chubby as a toddler with wrinkles at her wrists and thighs that looked like she'd wrapped her legs in hair elastics. Whenever I went to HP's house to see her, she'd be dancing to tunes from *The Little Mermaid* or clapping homemade play dough between plum-thick fingers. She ran right into my arms the second I arrived.

At Christmas three years back, Saskia was threading tree decorations made out of pasta. On the floor Olive drew an oversized snowman on a wide sheet of paper, coloring his scarf outside the lines with a gold-glitter crayon.

"She has her dad's temperament," Saskia said. She tilted her head the way mothers do when all they can see in the world is their own beautiful creation. In the background, ABBA played on a continuous loop.

"She's lucky to be like HP," I said, then added, "And you."

"We all are lucky and so, so blessed." Saskia got up from the breakfast counter and put her arm around my shoulders. Her touch baffled me, made me feel like plastic.

"Are you like HP?" I inched along the countertop so that my rib cage separated from hers.

"Hamish and I are peas in a pod," she said. "I feel so lucky that we see life the same way: as a journey, a

188

series of amazing adventures. Anything's possible once you figure that out. Don't you think?"

I couldn't answer. I've never had assurance like hers.

I babysat for HP and Saskia whenever they needed, and the more I did, the more Saskia confided in me. After a while she got real. She went into great, un-requested detail about how having a baby can really drive a wedge between a husband and a wife, and how impotant it was to secure a "date night" just to stay in touch. She seemed desperate for a confidante and per-haps believed that telling me all her deepest thoughts and fears was a currency with which she might buy my allegiance.

One night last August, I sat with Olive at bedtime. As she liked to remind me, she was starting preschool in the fall like a big girl, so whenever I was over at her house we had to practice reading all the time. HP and Saskia were at the movies, watching some flick about love and time travel—Saskia's pick. For some reason, Olive had had a meltdown when they were leaving, and I'd bribed her with candy. Finally she was calm, exhausted, just in time for bed. Olive's hands were still sticky from the candy, even after I'd washed her up.

"I feel a bit sweaty," she said, turning pages of her storybook, a mindless tale about a ballerina mouse.

"Do we have to read this book?" I asked. "It's super lame."

"Superlame-o!" shouted Olive, as if it were a new cartoon character. "Mommy gave this book to me."

"Do you like your mommy?" I asked.

"She's pretty."

"Who do you like more—her or me?"

Olive turned her hot little face up towards mine and planted her hand on my forearm. She sighed a breath of overripe strawberries. "Am I pretty, Angie?" she asked, her eyes suddenly, inexplicably, brimming with tears.

"You *are*. You are so, so pretty." I put my arm around her and handed her another candy from my pocket.

"But I already brushed my teeth," she whispered.

"We won't tell anyone. It can be our little secret."

chapter
17

"Why tell me that?" asks Novak.

"What?"

"Why tell me you manipulated the mind of a child?"

"Are you going to arrest me for giving a kid candy and telling her she's beautiful?"

Novak walks around the room. Under the electric light, he looks haunted. "Can we talk more about where you were two nights ago, Angela?"

"What's *your* first name? You use mine all the time, in almost every sentence. What's yours?"

There's a second or two of wariness. "Jonah."

"Oh, my God. I wouldn't have guessed that."

"Where were you the afternoon of June fifteenth?"

"What was the fifteenth—Thursday? I was at my house, or rather my mom's. We covered that already . . . Jonah."

Novak sits down. "Tell me what you know, Angela. Now. So, you were at home on Thursday evening?"

"I went home after work, ate dinner in my kitchen and went to sleep on the couch."

"I thought you were living at the Parkers' house while you gave your mother space to adapt."

"Like I said, I moved into HP's for a while. And then I moved out again."

He pauses, then reefs through his notes, bookmarking a page with a hooked thumb. "Mr. Parker says you lived with them for six weeks. When did you move out?"

"Didn't he say? Oh, it was a couple of weeks ago, I believe. Early June."

"Is that when you stole Saskia's necklace?"

"I told you. I don't know anything about that. Olive must have put it in my book. You know how kids are always hiding things."

"I need the details of why you moved out. Full disclosure."

"Well, pick a direction, Jonah. One minute you're telling me to hurry the fuck up, the next minute you're asking for more detail."

He weighs every word when he speaks. "Just tell me what I need to know."

"Oh, Jonah," I say. "You need to trust that I'm steering you for a reason. I'm taking you all the way to the middle of the maze. Can't you see how easy this is for you? All you've ever had to do was listen."

When I called HP and told him that I was stuck living with my mother, he was quick to offer me his place to stay.

"I saw your mom downtown, actually. She told me all about it. What if you come our way for a bit, stay with us?" His voice was eager. "We'll cheer you up. We've got the room, and nobody wants to live with their parents."

"Yours would be okay."

"Everyone has their . . . quirks." He paused on the word. "When you live with them."

"So I won't be in the way?"

"Little J—" He faltered. "Angela. You're family."

He didn't even check with Saskia first, or at least I don't think he did. When I turned up the next day, they put me in their spare room at the top of a curving staircase, every solid step of which HP had sanded into smooth, pale wood. Most of the walls in the house were blue—the kind of aqua you see in postcards sent from the Greek islands. It was as if Saskia were trying to paint herself into the ocean she'd long ago given up.

Above the fireplace, they'd framed a huge photograph of themselves bungee jumping from a bridge in New Zealand. Their ankles were tied together, and at the moment when the camera had captured them, they were at the pinnacle of their bounce, the strain in their spines identical.

HP's house faced west, so that every evening Saskia sat on the porch and watched the sun dip behind the smoothness of the mountains, casting oily shadows onto the horizon of the lake. She called 5 p.m. "sundowners" and claimed it as adult time, always making popcorn and dusting it sparingly with sea salt and flakes of nutritional yeast. She handed out Australian lager in tall cans. HP and I were expected to attend.

"I'm stoked you're staying with us, Ange," Saskia chirped that first evening. "No point worrying your mum. Stay as long as you like, mate, no worries." She reached across the swing seat and bumped me on top of my wrist. Bullfrogs sang in the ditches. "So, go on then—what's the deal with your oldies?"

That was the thing about Saskia: she loved gossip. I took a swig of my lager, denting the can's Australian flag with my thumb. "You know," I began, "most people get married because they can't think of anything else to do."

HP stopped whittling the stick he had in his lap and looked up at me.

194

"I guess my mom only just figured that out."

"They weren't soul mates, she and your dad?" Saskia put her hand to her chest, sighing with an empathy I doubt she actually felt.

"There's no such thing."

HP laughed and shook his head.

"What, you don't believe in true love?" Saskia looked crestfallen.

"I believe most people get together because it's easier to fight off desolation in pairs. There's no end to the drivel you can talk about if you have someone to bounce words off. Marriage is the easiest way in the world to stay distracted—you can literally waste hours on the couch while one of you channel-surfs on behalf of the other."

"That's sad," said Saskia. "That's a heaps dark perspective."

"I call bullshit." HP wagged his knife at me. "As *if* you don't believe in soul mates. You talked of nothing else in high school."

I glared at him from the padded swing seat and pushed it back suddenly. Saskia jerked forwards. "Sorry," I said to her. Then I walked away, into the house.

HP knew what I was thinking: if soul mates are real, how can it be that Saskia and I both have the same one?

There was only one answer: one of us was lying.

Saskia disappeared between five forty-five and six forty-five every night, scurrying inside to cook for and feed and bathe and clothe and rock and soothe and sing to and settle her five-year-old. She called it the "witching hour," Saskia's term for Olive's ability to turn into a purple screaming monster, although in my opinion the witching hour referred to Saskia herself, because at that time every day she was worn out. Neither I nor HP could ask her a question without having our sentence snapped short by terseness.

"Do you need any help with the . . ." I'd begin, or, "Where did you put the . . ." only to have Saskia wheel around on me with a half-chopped banana and a face on fire. After some time I caught on to the rhythms of her mood schedule and knew, like HP, that the best way to get through witching hour was to stay away. Often HP joined me.

"I thought she loved being a mom," I muttered one evening as HP and I watched her slam clothes into the washing machine.

"She does. But it's not easy. Everyone has their moments."

"Every day?"

We both laughed, the way people do when they're not saying what they really think. More and more, I realized that HP was describing their life together in terms other than perfection and paradise. One night, as I read late in the spare room, I could hear Saskia crying softly at the bottom of the stairs. HP was down there, too. I tiptoed to the landing and stood in the shadows near the top step.

"Quit stressing so much," HP was saying. I could see the crown of his head as he crouched near Saskia's knees. "We've got a lifetime of this ahead of us; it's a marathon, not a sprint."

"I'm never present enough. I keep losing things. I left Olive's stuffy at the mall."

"Again?" he said.

"Yes. We went back for it." She sniffed. "I just can't be all things to all people."

"You're doing fine. You're an amazing mom." He reached out and lifted her chin. "Olive's happy and thriving. She's doing great."

"You're so happy-go-lucky. I wish I was like that."

Just as they paused in their whispering, the cell in my back pocket started to ring and I flew back into the spare room, swearing under my breath.

"Hello?"

"Darling? What's the matter? You sound flustered." My mother was pouring herself a drink. I could hear the flap of liquid in the background.

"It's kind of late, Mom. What is it that you want?"

"Want?" She sipped and spoke through a wash of

liquor. I could picture her lips containing the tide. "Can't I call my only daughter for a chat? Goodness. I'm calling to tell you you're welcome to move back here, darling, whenever you like. I'd love some company."

My mind raced. I wasn't ready to leave.

"Honestly, I can't believe you sleep a wink in that house with a married couple and a child. You've given me a nice break, but maybe it's time to come home."

A break? What was that supposed to mean? I didn't want to go back. I was fine where I was. "I don't know, Mom."

"If there's some tension over there, HP and Saskia probably need some space. Because let me tell you something I've learned: nobody's happy. You mark my words—*nobody*."

"Have you heard from Dad?"

She didn't answer. I could just hear her breath and the ice in her glass clinking.

"Or don't you have any friends you could invite over for a few days?" I asked. "What happened to all the ladies from harp class?"

"It's not . . . I don't need company, darling. That's not it. I just think this is the right place for you right now."

"Okay, Mom. I'll be there . . . soon. I just have to help out here for a few more days."

"If you must, Angela," she continued quietly, "although I'm not sure it's healthy."

I wasn't clear if she meant for me or for her, but either way I didn't hurry to move back in with my mom. I couldn't. I didn't want to be her caregiver or look after her while she went through her melodramatic upheaval. She was milking it: she'd been the one to leave Dad. If anyone needed company, it was more likely him. But Dad was a dog that had been hit by a car: he'd limped to the coast and wouldn't emerge until he'd gotten past the worst of his injuries. And in the meantime I had a new family. I was a godmother to Olive now. It was something I was getting good at.

"You're nesting," Freddy joked every time we spoke or he drove up to Cove to take me out for dinner. "Two's company, you know, or are you unfamiliar with the age-old adages?"

Of course I wasn't at HP's house all the time in those weeks. Work kept me at the office weekdays from eight thirty until four, and on the weekends Saskia was always rushing off to mommy groups or playdates or teach-your-kid-to-be-amazing-at-everything sessions. I did spend a few Friday nights in New York with Freddy, listening to jazz in his apartment and eating food so elaborate he must have ordered in. He asked me questions about HP but never seemed to care about my answers, glazing over as he opened fresh bottles of wine.

Freddy and my mother might have wanted me out of the Parker house, but the longer I stayed, the more comfortable I felt there. HP, Saskia and I ate dinner every night in their echoing dining room, a twinkly old chandelier hanging over our heads. Olive was squared away to bed by that point in the evening. The table could easily seat ten, so each meal felt a bit like a board meeting, but still, it was something. Saskia would pop up from her chair to put on new iPad playlists that she'd compiled during the day. She liked songs that made me think of seventeen-year-olds road-tripping to California in a convertible. I've never felt so buoyed while eating. Saskia's mood seemed to dull whenever HP and I joked and laughed together. He'd whip side dishes down the table towards me, making some in-joke or other. Her grimaces were momentary, however, and she regrouped with new conversation starters, as if she had cue cards hidden in her lap.

"If you were a color, what color would you be?"

"Do you believe in magic?"

"What is the happiest moment of your life so far?"

They were questions straight out of a Grade 9 sleepover. Eventually Saskia ran out of prompts, so the subject at dinner conversation rarely strayed from

Olive—what she said that day, what new milestone she'd reached, what she had for breakfast. Since there was only so much I could absorb of Olive's daily successes, I began to bring photographs to the dinner table, just to change the pace. I unearthed a steady stream of classic shots from Grade 11 parties and grad, mostly to get HP smiling. It was like a mini high school reunion every night. We laughed out loud at the ridiculousness of our old Halloween costumes or the height of Ezra's hair during his teenage years.

"Who's the girl?" Saskia responded to just about every photo she looked at.

"I gave up counting," HP said, "and so should you."

"He doesn't discriminate very well," I explained.

"He *didn't*," Saskia said.

I scanned the credenza for more wine. When HP went to help Saskia carry dishes back into the kitchen, he punched me on the arm, unseen by her. I could hear Saskia in the kitchen as she dropped cutlery into the sink, the pitch of her voice a mosquito-whine, until finally HP came back and told me to quit it with the photographs.

"It makes her feel left out," he said.

That night I stuck all the pictures into a photo album. It was probably a mistake to leave it on the coffee table in the living room.

Shortly after that, Saskia invited Ezra over for

dinner. The inference was that he hadn't come over in a while.

"On a Friday night?" HP asked when he heard of Ezra's invitation. "You're brave."

Saskia spent the whole afternoon cooking a vegetarian dish made with red peppers that she kept calling capsicums. By the time Ezra showed up it was past 8 p.m., and he'd brought a guest with him. From the look on Saskia's face, he'd not mentioned he was going to bring anyone. Saskia scurried to lay another place at the dining room table.

"Uh-oh," said HP when he opened the door. Both Ezra and the woman he'd brought had that sloping gait of alcohol and afternoon sun. Ezra's youthful good looks were a little the worse for wear, sure, but she looked mid-forties. The closer she got, the more of a squint she developed. All but three buttons of her shirt were undone.

"We late?" Ezra licked his teeth. HP held the screen door open for them. "Thanks, buddy. Sorry, we got sidetracked."

"Ezra!" Saskia arrived at the door again and stood behind HP and me. "I'm afraid you've missed Olive, she's already—"

"You're looking ravishing, Saskia. Tidy as always."

"Are you hungry?" she asked. "You look like you could use some food."

As she walked back towards the kitchen, she raised both eyebrows at HP, like it was him that was wasted.

Ezra burped through dinner and barely touched his food. He made reference to the fifteen or so wedding photos Saskia had hung on the wall, noting his absence in all of them. Every now and then HP told him to behave, but the animosity was palpable.

"So what are your plans, Ezra?" Saskia chewed a small mouthful of peppers. "Did you get any more swim-tryout-offer things?"

"Water polo," Ez said. "And I didn't make the cut. That's okay, Saskia, life's full of losers. We can't all be perfect."

"Watch it," said HP, pointing with his knife. "I'm not telling you again."

"Haym?" Saskia's head tilted. "Settle down. It's nice to have mates over. Let's not spoil good tucker."

HP got up then, and took a long time in the kitchen finding a beer.

After we'd made it through dinner, I drove Ezra and his date home. We took off down the north shore, Ezra next to me in the passenger seat, his window wound down as he howled like a wolf in the night air. We were almost in town by the time he turned to face me. "I still fucking hate Saskia."

I exhaled and switched gears.

"She took him right out from under us, LJ. When

I first met her, I thought she was going to be a good thing." He squinted into the rearview mirror. In the backseat his date was fast asleep. "You remember my old dog in high school? Renfield, you called him, needy as shit, crazy, followed me from room to room?"

I nodded and turned left.

"You know what I figured out lately? Saskia is Renfield. She's everywhere, always whining, pawing, desperate to help." He grimaced. "I hated that dog. Wanted it gone." He paused. "Here, this is me."

I pulled up outside a ragged apartment building with a paneled door smeared with a thousand fingerprints.

"You wanna come up? Have a coffee? Make out?" He fumbled his way out of the car and opened the rear door, pulling at the arm of his girlfriend. "Or whatever, turn me down. It wouldn't be the first time." He crouched in the gap of the passenger door while his date toppled out.

"Ez, whatever happened to your dog?"

"Got hit by a car," he said. "Still had to pay to get it put down."

I drove back to HP's house and opened the door quietly. Saskia was on the couch in the living room, HP beside her.

204

"He's just lost," HP was saying. "He doesn't mean anything by it."

"He hates me. They all do. I can't get anything right. Even Angela—"

I walked straight into the living room.

"Hey," said HP, sitting up. "You get them back safely?"

"Yeah. Ezra was in a chatty mood."

Saskia looked at her feet. Olive cried out upstairs and Saskia jumped up as if an Olympic pistol had just fired, leaving HP and me alone.

I sat next to him on the couch. I don't know why, maybe I was thinking of those grad days, but I jabbed him in the ribs, play-fighting.

"What are you . . . ?" He batted me away, or maybe he was going to start a tickle fight, but just then Saskia appeared in the doorway holding Olive.

"Babe?" Her face was flushed. "I need you; her bed needs changing."

HP pushed me away and stood. He strode out of the living room without even looking back.

I couldn't fall asleep that night, so I wandered downstairs in the darkness. I've always liked the quiet in a house when everyone else is sleeping. Houses take on a life of their own in the early hours of the morning: the hum of the fridge increasing to fill the absence of voices; the fabric of furniture lush to the fingertips;

floorboards primed to release sound. I moved around like a chess piece, stepping this way and that, my feet finding the parts of the floor I knew were noiseless. Through the living room window, the moon shone high over the smooth lake. The water rolled like mercury, thick and viscous.

One of Olive's stuffed toys lay slumped on the windowsill, so after a while I went up to her room to return it. Dusky light striped the stairway through the window. How soft the steps were under my feet, the broad strokes of HP's shoulders and hands having smoothed the wood. A children's book lay on Olive's bedroom floor, ready to read for tomorrow. *Are You My Mother?* the title read. I stepped around it to the side of the bed.

"Olive," I whispered. A crescent of brown skin peeped out from where her pajama top had ridden up. Her belly button rose and fell. "Olive, move over."

I lay my body along the warmth of her. She turned and threw a short arm around my neck. We lay like that for a minute. Then she opened her eyes, blinking and rubbing at her nose with a knuckled fist.

"Where's Mommy?" she asked.

"Next door, sleeping. Can I lie in here with you for a bit?"

"You can have Chops." She found a rag-doll lamb and placed him alongside my neck. "Mom says I'm a big girl and I need to sleep in my own bed."

"She's right. You are a big girl."

"You are, too. But I won't tell."

We slept like that until dawn, when I slipped back to my own room.

A few days after Ezra's disastrous dinner party, I walked in from work to find Saskia and Olive coloring princess castles at the dining room table. They both looked up when I entered, brushing blond hair from their brows in perfect synchronicity.

"Where's HP?" I asked. I was hungry and opened the fridge.

"Baseball practice. Their team's killing it. It's so exciting."

He played in a beer league, slow-pitch, on the same team as Ezra. They had a game every Saturday afternoon, a thinly veiled excuse to go to the bar every Saturday night from May to September.

When I took a can of soda pop from the fridge, Olive's eyebrows shot up. "You want one?" I asked her.

"No, thank you!" Saskia chimed on Olive's behalf. She didn't look up from the coloring, moving her golden pen within the lines. I wandered over to their table and sat down. She clicked the lid of the pen back on and stood up, brushing her hands on the front of her frayed jean shorts.

"Let's go for a walk! Come on, all of us. It's beautiful outside."

"What, now?" I'd just walked in the door.

"It'll be fun. Olive, get your bike. You can ride the lakeside path, and Godmother Angie and I will walk."

It was only a block to the beach, and the path around the lake was paved smooth enough that Olive could easily pedal on it, although she needed help getting going. Her bicycle helmet had pink bunny rabbits along its edges, and glittery plastic tassels hung from the handlebars, clacking in the wind as she rode.

I took my soda with me and drank it as we walked. As soon as Olive was up ahead of us, Saskia launched her question.

"How long do you think you'll stay with us?" Her tone was light. "I know your mom is eager for you to go home . . ."

I scrunched my can and threw it in the recycle bin. "How do you know that?"

She threaded her arm through mine, throwing me off-stride. "Ange, can I ask you something?"

I unlinked my arm before I spoke. "Go ahead. I won't bite."

"Do you think you and I could be friends?" From there it was a flood, a torrent. "I mean, I know we get on and everything, but I've been thinking about it heaps lately, and I want to be close with you like Haym is—you know, the kind of friendship you can count on. I see how you feel about him."

I looked at her carefully. Her eyes were wide, her palms open as she spoke. I said nothing.

"I mean you guys have a history—you've known each other much longer than I've—"

"Eleven years."

"Gosh. I'm only at seven." Saskia took a breath. "Okay, well, what I'm saying is I'd like that for us, too. For you and me." She stopped walking and blinked at me with summer-sky eyes. She looked like a child at a magic show, watching the handkerchief, waiting for the pure white dove.

Up ahead, Olive wobbled to a stop. She pointed at a tree and yelled something that the wind whipped across the lake. Saskia waved and gave her a thumbs-up. When she turned to me, she seemed more confident.

"Sometimes I think we met on the same night because of fate. I mean, if you'd told me in that beer tent in Oxford that one day we'd all be living in the same house on a beautiful lake, walking on a cool evening with my daughter playing in front of us—well . . . It just proves things work out as they should."

"Seems too good to be true."

"It's just a dream of mine to have a woman I can talk to, trust. I've always known the universe would look after me. I know we can be closer."

Just then Olive got too tired to pedal and Saskia had to push the bike all the way home with her back half bent. There was no more conversation, no more girl talk. We walked home in the dusk and it was then that I knew how this story would turn out. On the lake, a dark wave gathered, stretching and flexing. Soon it would flood, slipping under the doorways of her house and seeping into every window, turning every wall from blue to black.

The universe was coming for her and nobody saw it but me.

chapter

18

"Is Saskia's disappearance the ending you're referring to, Angela?" Novak asks.

"Maybe it's the real world teaching her a lesson."

"That's cold."

"Perhaps." I refuse to give more.

He sits back, disgusted. "We found your big glass jar, you know."

It takes me a minute to figure out what he might be talking about, and immediately my mouth floods with bile. "What big glass jar?"

"The one in your closet, Angela, dusty and hidden up high behind yearbooks and grad memorabilia. Your 'Manifestations Jar.'" He makes air quotes around the phrase. "Did you think we wouldn't find it?"

"That's not mine. It can't be. I threw it out years ago." My goddamn mother. Why would she have pulled that from the trash? "Mom must have salvaged it," I say.

"Interesting. So your mom rescued your *manifest destiny*."

The catchphrase shocks me. Did my mother give him that? I shift in my seat, smooth a wrinkle out of my pant fabric. "The jar was her idea. It was a dumb teenage thing. Whatever's in there isn't mine anymore, Novak."

"Whatever's in there is handwritten, committed to paper. I told you, it makes things so much easier for us," he says.

"You can't use the thoughts I had as a nineteen-year-old kid against me! That's ridiculous." My brain races, trying to remember what I might have written down.

"They're bringing the jar in. We'll take a look then, shall we? At the very least, it'll be a nice walk down memory lane."

"I want a lawyer."

"I was wondering when you'd ask."

We'd come so far together, I didn't want Novak to leave just yet. It's strange, the attachments we form in spite of ourselves. And besides, I hadn't told him enough of the story. I hadn't even told him about the big fight; I knew he'd want to hear about it. I picked up from a few days before the first weekend in June, when HP told me that Saskia's book club and his baseball game were both the coming Saturday.

"I don't mind watching Olive," I offered. "I'll just be here reading anyway."

"No Freddy this weekend? That's a drag." HP rinsed a dinner plate and handed it to me to dry and put away.

"I'm meeting him next weekend in Boston. He's paying for everything. This Saturday he's at a conference in Virginia."

"Of course he is. Up there, left-hand side." He nodded at a cupboard and then pointed with his elbow, his hands still in the water.

"It's on smuggling opiates undetected across borders."

"That'd be cool if it was anyone else. That guy couldn't do anything undetected."

I glanced sideways at HP. "I think Freddy's just expected to know about it; I'm sure he hasn't done it himself."

"Yeah, well." HP swirled the sponge over another plate. "I get the feeling he probably has some firsthand experience with illegal activity that he hasn't disclosed.

You can't work with chemical warfare and remain completely innocent."

I weighed what he said but didn't speak. Upstairs Saskia's footsteps creaked on the floorboards outside Olive's bedroom, and HP looked up at the ceiling.

"Nobody's innocent anymore." I slowly clipped the old cupboard door closed. "It doesn't matter what job you do: it's a rite of passage."

"What does that mean?"

"We've all gotten older. It's impossible to do that without taking damage, or causing it."

He turned to face me then, his arms hanging by his sides. Suds dripped from his fingertips onto the tiled floor.

"I can't ever tell what you're getting at lately."

"I'm not getting at anything."

"You're just . . ." He threw out one hand so that small drops of water splattered against the wall. "You're so negative about everything. Sometimes you're a real downer."

"HP, in my experience—"

"Oh, change the tune. Seriously. All you know are death marches."

I stepped with my hand on the kitchen door. "I can't believe you think that about me."

"You've been churning out misery for a decade. Can't you see that we feel sorry for you? All of us?"

All of us? What was that supposed to even mean? With his back to the door, he couldn't see my eyes burning into the back of his skull. I kept my voice level. "If I'm so difficult to be around, do you even want me to babysit?"

"Yes. Olive likes you. We decided long ago to include you in our family, to take the high road, to try to help you. But it would be a lot easier if you didn't act like Eeyore in Olive's *Winnie-the-Pooh* book." Despite the wisecrack, he didn't turn around. I slinked out and on the way up the stairs passed Saskia.

"Going to bed already?" Shadows from the landing window wisped across her composed face, even at night she glowed. "Are you okay?"

I laughed. "HP and I had a fight. He's being an asshole. It's nothing."

She sighed. It sounded maternal and made me gag. "Well, sometimes that happens. It's best to just sleep it off and it'll all be all right in the morning."

"You talk like you know him better than me," I said.

Her face screwed up into a question mark. "I'm his wife. Of course I *know* him."

"Do you know about Thomson?"

Her eyes shot up as if jolted.

There it was. Real, faltering doubt. HP hadn't told his wife about his poor dead brother. She looked about to cry.

"Listen," I said. "Forget about that. All I'm saying is that wives, husbands—for a lot of people it's nothing but a job description and there's always the hope of promotion."

Saskia placed her arm carefully on the railing and moved down one step past me. "Is this what you and Hamish were fighting about—you bringing up the institution of marriage again?"

"No. HP and I were disputing more important things." She still wouldn't walk all the way down the stairs. "Look, everything's fine. Apparently, it doesn't matter what I think or what I say."

"Maybe stop talking all the time, then," she snapped.

"Excuse me?"

She lifted her chin. "Just shut up a little bit. Nobody would mind." It took everything she had to say it. It was like a choir girl swearing in church.

I reached down and patted her on the shoulder. "That's more like it, Saskia! Good for you. At last you show up to the fight."

I return my mind to the present. I've been entirely honest with Novak, so my conscience is clean. I don't know if he'll believe it, but HP never once apologized. Not for anything. You'd think if a guy made a series of wrong turns, he'd eventually stop driving the car

216

and get out. Not HP. The next morning was Friday and when I woke for work, I could hear him grinding coffee beans in the kitchen. It was June so his timetable was more relaxed, but he always got up and made breakfast before going for a run. Olive didn't usually wake until close to eight and since Saskia's whole existence was dictated by motherhood duty, her clock was linked entirely to her daughter's. She rarely made an appearance until after I'd left. If I timed it right, I could usually catch HP alone for a solid twenty minutes before I had to get to the office.

He turned when I walked into the kitchen and then carried on grinding his coffee. He was barefoot, in shorts and a tank top as usual. Early summer had darkened his shoulder blades. I slid into a chair at the breakfast counter and readjusted the bust of my shirt.

He came over and stood opposite me, bringing a cup filled to the brim with steaming coffee.

"You want some, you can help yourself," he said.

"I'm good. They have coffee at work."

He watched me for a few seconds before speaking—long enough that I felt the color rise in the skin around my throat. "So you and my wife had quite the little chat last night."

I licked my lips. "Did we?"

"You've no right to use my family's tragedy as part of your little game."

"I didn't. I just said your brother's name, is all."

"Why can't you just grow up, Angela? Everything's a test to see who I like more. Is there anything you want to ask me? Anything you don't understand?"

I shook my head.

"Good. Because I'd hate to think you're harboring some old resentment. Life's too short." His expression relaxed a little, and he took another sip of coffee. "There are things about me that only you know. You have that—it's yours. You don't need to keep proving it to everyone."

He looked at me, a look I didn't understand. "You can't live here forever. You can't keep relying on us to dig you out of a hole. Go have some fun for once in your life."

The kitchen door opened and Saskia walked in wearing HP's robe and carrying Olive.

"Honey, I was just saying to Angela that it's time for her to go. No problem or anything, no fight; just time to move on."

Saskia gripped her daughter close. "Of course, you're always welcome to visit. Drop by at sundowners. Olive would love to see you." All three sentences were of identical flatness and weight, doled out like dinner plates.

"Angela's leaving? No!" shouted Olive. Everyone pretended they hadn't heard her.

"I'll be gone by Sunday. Is that fast enough?" I stood up from my chair, smoothing out my clothes.

"Of course. Thanks for understanding," Saskia said.

I went straight to my car and called my mom. She let her phone ring for a while before picking up. "Mom, can I come home?"

"Oh, sweetheart," she gushed like a high wind down the line, "of course you can come home. It's been deathly dull here, and I'll be happy to see you back."

"They've asked me to leave."

"HP has?" Why didn't she sound more surprised?

"I think it's more Saskia. But yes." My voice caught and I coughed to conceal it.

"Angela Petitjean, don't you dare cry. Don't you dare. You've been doing great. Don't let this pull you down. Do you want me to come and get you?"

"I'm on my way to work. And I'm not leaving until Sunday."

"Sunday? Why not today?"

"They need me to babysit tomorrow night."

"Are you joking?" Her voice was hard and flat. "Is that a joke?"

"Just—it's okay, Mom. I want to do it. You know how much I care about Olive."

"Whatever you think is best, Angela. But you give too much, you know. Soon you'll have nothing left."

I stayed in my room that Friday night and spent

219

most of Saturday at work, sorting through registrations of births and deaths. There was no reason for me to put in overtime, other than that I didn't want to be anywhere else.

Saskia was ready for book club by the time I got back to their place. She waited in clothes more suited for clubbing, and didn't direct any conversation my way. Finally, she'd given up pretending that she liked me.

"You got everything you need?" HP stood by the screen door once his wife had left, waiting for Ez to pick him up for baseball.

"I've babysat before." I sat in an armchair, and Olive crawled into my lap.

"Okay, well, you have my cell if anything goes wrong."

"We'll be fine, won't we, pumpkin?" I stood up, looping my arms around Olive's legs and carrying her in front of me. "Let's find some food! Then it's bath. Then it's bedtime." I waddled his daughter out of sight through the swing door into the kitchen as Ezra's truck pulled up, the bass bumping from the stereo.

"Thanks for doing this, LJ," HP called after me as he grabbed his door keys.

I didn't respond. Instead, I pulled out the bottle of New Zealand Pinot Noir they'd been saving for a special occasion and sliced at its neck with a paring knife.

Once Olive had eaten enough, I ran her a bath and sent her to find pajamas and a hairbrush. I don't know why, but I wandered into HP and Saskia's bedroom with my glass of wine. How had I never noticed the scarlet throw Saskia draped across the white comforter, the tea candles scattered on every windowsill, the fairy lights over the dark oak headboard? She'd hung themed pictures of trees, all of them cone-shaped and Tuscan-looking, though she'd never been to Italy.

Her jewelry box overflowed with long-stringed pendants—feathers, arrows, keys—and bulbous rings. Behind that was a cluster of lavish perfume bottles.

"Godmother Angie," Olive said suddenly behind me, and I jumped to find her in the doorway. Her belly was nut brown against the yellow fabric of her underpants. "What are you doing in here?"

"Oh, just looking."

"I'm not allowed," she confided, padding over to me in her bare feet. "Mommy says I mustn't touch her jewels."

"I won't tell if you won't."

Olive pulled down the jewelry case from the dresser, standing on tiptoes with her tongue sticking out. Once she had the box in both hands, she crouched and set it on the carpet. "Which one's the best?" Her chubby fingers played with the silver strings, ran over the smoothness of the pendants. "I think this one." She held up an elephant pendant on a chain, her dark eyes watching the light as it caught on the jade and aqua.

"It's pretty. Your mom has a thing for elephants." I hated the necklace. It took me straight back to that beer tent at the May Ball.

"Mom says elephants are good at being sad." Olive folded the silver necklace into the small curve of her palm. "You have it." She held her closed hand out to me.

"No, Olive. Thank you, but no."

"Mommy would like you to have it. She says it's nice to cheer people up."

I wanted to laugh, long and loud and dry, but instead I pushed her hand away gently. "Put it back. Good girl. Now give me a hug—there, that's a great one—and go find your hairbrush. Wait for me in the bathroom; don't get in."

I watched her trot away and picked up my wineglass, sipping as I surveyed more of the room.

There were no signs that HP slept in there. No baseball caps, no watches, no shorts left crumpled by his side of the bed. To the side of me was a heavy, beach-washed dresser; I slid open the top left drawer. Here were Saskia's socks, paired at the neck with a decisive fold, two by two. I closed that drawer.

The one below was double the size and harder to open. Inside lay all the T-shirts, ironed flat and nudging shoulders. Burrowing in between them, I dug farther, looking for some sign of their marriage that wasn't humdrum. A pair of handcuffs, zebra-furred? A blindfold? Leather? Didn't every couple have some secret hidden away in a corner of their room?

The top right drawer held all of Saskia's underwear: I dipped my hands into the softness, letting the fabric fold like water over my fingertips. Pulling out a pair—pink with a chocolate ribbon and lace around the stitching—I reached up under my skirt and gently tugged my own underwear down, rolling them off into a straight line by my bare feet. The slipperiness of the new silk fabric slid against my thighs. I turned around and stared at my reflection in the long pine mirror by the wardrobe. The sight made me giggle: my butt looked pert and perfectly hoisted by the expensive cut of the cloth. Two steps backwards and I pressed my flesh to the mirror, leaving a round crescent imprint on the glass. Before I straightened my skirt and walked back out towards the bathroom, I kicked my old underwear under their bed, wrong-side out.

The bath was ready. Olive came in with her pajamas and a hairbrush piled above the level of her chin and I sat her into the piping-hot water and gave her the cork from the Pinot Noir. She prodded it with her forefinger, trying to make it sink. Now and again she stood to stamp on it with her bobbly toes, exposing a ring around her plum belly where the bottom half of her body glowed hotter.

"Wash everywhere," I said as she made a beard out of bath foam.

"I'm Santa," she said, peering at her mirrored face in the shiny disk below the tap. "Do you believe in Santa?"

My wineglass already needed a refill. "Santa is to kids what God is to grown-ups. We all need bedtime stories to keep ourselves cozy."

She stood suddenly and slapped her round, red belly with both wrinkly hands. On the rack were three fluffy white towels, each embroidered with a first-name initial in the lower left corner. I rolled my eyes and grabbed the S one. Olive clambered out of the bath and I wrapped her up. I made sure to dry her well.

"Can I have a bedtime story to keep me cozy?" She stepped her rosy knees into her matching pajama bottoms, which were covered with owls.

"Sure. I've got lots in my head."

She crawled into bed quickly, curling with her hands pressed palm-to-palm under her cheek. I pulled the blanket over her and turned off her Tinker Bell lamp so that shadows from the landing light split her ceiling.

"Once upon a time," I said, stroking the white-blond strands of hair at the crest of her forehead, "there was a little girl who grew up by a lake. She was a pretty girl and very clever. Everybody loved her."

"Does anyone die in this story?" Olive rasped. Her eyes were closed.

"I'm not sure yet. When the little girl was born, her mom and dad were the proudest parents in the land. They threw a huge party with cake and balloons and sparklers. But at the party an evil, jealous witch snuck in and she poisoned the cake and her mom ate it and fell down asleep for five whole years."

"The mom was poisoned?" She was captured the way kids always are with dark stories.

"For five whole years she was asleep and the witch took the place of the mom and tricked the little girl and the daddy."

"How did she trick them?"

"By pretending she was the mom."

Olive opened her eyes. Her little-girl tummy pressed against her pajama top. "Does the real mom wake up and kill the witch and the family lives happily ever after, The End?"

"Well, life's not always like that."

Olive sighed sweet hot breath towards my face and rolled over, tumbling nearer to sleep. "Poor God-mother Angie," she mumbled.

"Why poor me?"

"There's a mommy and a daddy. You're the witch."

"I'm not the witch! Why am I the witch?"

But she'd fallen asleep. I left her room quietly, my face hot with injustice.

Novak's pager beeps and he stands up jerkily. "There's someone who wants to see you." His exit is rushed like a new idea.

chapter
19

When the door to the interview room opens again I expect it to be Novak with my mom. It's the kind of move he'd make: drag the parent into the principal's office to make the disappointing kid feel worse.

But it's not her.

HP walks the few steps to the chair alone, and my stomach twists with a longing to hug him. His flip-flops clack. I haven't seen him for two weeks and he looks tired and frayed, although he's recently shaved.

"Hi." He doesn't smile, but he's not giving off rage, either. "Are they treating you okay?"

"Yeah. I'm sorry about Saskia," I say.

He nods slowly and gives me another look I can't

read. "LJ, I know it's crazy, but I can't help thinking that she's left me. You know, just walked out."

"That's what I keep telling Novak!"

"Yeah, you get it. And you know what? Maybe she was right to. I mean, we've been having some . . . Well, it doesn't matter, but this kind of shock gets a guy to thinking. We should have spent more time together, you and me."

My breath catches in my throat. This is all I've ever wanted.

"I'm sorry about stuff I did to you in Oxford and all the years since."

I daren't exhale. There's a flood buried inside me. I'm a well no one's looked into for years.

I take a deep, steadying breath. I hadn't expected an apology. "What are you going to do about Saskia? I mean, when they find her or she comes back?"

He looks towards the door, then at his feet. "Novak told me he has a new lead. Do you know anything that could help him?"

There it is. At the very center of his soft blue eyes, I can see the truth, the pickax metal hatred he's trying to hide.

"You fucking bastard," I say.

He sits back and flounders. "LJ, what do you—?"

"You come in here and manipulate me?"

228

"She's my wife, Angela. And she's disappeared. Do you understand what that even means?"

"Does that give you a right to lie to me? To manipulate me? Oh, Novak must have thought it was a masterstroke, sending you in here. Who's to say you didn't hurt her yourself?"

He's suddenly glacial, his eyes cold. When he launches, it's feral how fast he moves. He has one hand around my throat before my chair even tips back, before it clatters to the floor. Part of me is excited by the swiftness with which he grabs me, but I can hardly get air.

"Where's my wife?" he yells.

My feet are off the floor now, my eyes bulging and wet. The door flings open and Novak and a couple of cops barrel in behind him. It takes all of them to pull HP off me. When the white of his fingertips finally slips from the skin of my throat, I slide down the wall, my lungs raking. Novak speaks into HP's ear while I gasp for breath. I can't hear Novak's words but he calms HP down fast, then guides him out of the room, leaving me on the ground with the feel of HP's hands still on my skin.

chapter

20

I'm still trying to catch my breath when Novak comes back in, and as he takes his seat, he has just one question for me: *What did you do to make HP hate you this much?* But all I can think about are the years I've put aside for HP, all the times I've tried to show him how much I care. And still he doesn't know me. In the end, all roads lead to Saskia Parker, however hard I try. Whether or not Novak finds her, she isn't the great disappearance. She never was the most serious theft.

Novak, for his part, has been trying his best to follow the bread crumbs I've scattered along the way. At least he's making an effort. Maybe he deserves the rest of the story now. It's time to tell him what I did.

That Saturday night, my last at HP's, he didn't get in at nine like he said he would, and Saskia's book club ran even later. HP got in after ten and he was drunk. When I heard the fridge door clank open, I crept from the spare room to the top of the stairs.

A bottle cap clattered onto the tiling floor and I heard him sit with a sigh at the table and the sound of his bottle clunking the wood in between sips. When he stumbled up again, screeching the chair on the tiling, I quickly padded back to my room. From the crack in the hinges of my door, I saw him tiptoe to Olive's room. He swayed in the doorway, his shoulders and head craning forwards in the dusk. Then he bundled his way up the hall to his own room, nudging a framed picture with his shoulder as he passed it. I waited, then followed, watching from the door.

He'd gone to sleep so fast, his chest lifting and falling as he drifted with dreams. This poor, poor man. I crossed the threshold, thinking I'd better check that he wasn't so drunk that he'd vomit on himself. Maybe I should move him, so he wasn't in danger on his back. I knelt on his side of the bed, let his breath wash my face; if I timed it right, I could inhale everything he breathed out. I could smell the alcohol, potent on the fullness of his lips.

He hadn't changed so much over the years—a few laugh lines at the sides of his eyes and mouth. He'd thickened in the chest and shoulders, but his skin was as soft and olive-smooth. I ran my index finger down the side of his neck from his earlobe to his collarbone; he shifted his knees under the blanket.

I moved around the bed and by Saskia's table, lit by the glow of her digital clock, lifted my T-shirt and stood naked apart from the pink silk panties. I stretched, yawning my arms up so that my breasts cupped beautifully, my shadow silhouetted against the far wall. When I crawled under the covers, the sheets smelled like apricots, the weave rich and luxurious against my legs and ribs. For a second I lay quite still, living a moment of what should have been mine all along. My husband, my child, my house.

I slipped my hand across and over the wall of him, reached down into the cleft of his chest muscle and stroked fingertips along the broad swath of his stomach. My entire torso pressed against his back. Slowly I threaded my top leg around his, intertwining us at the calf and the thigh. His breath changed rhythm: he was surfacing. Leaning on my elbow, I breathed into the back of his neck, my nipples dusting his shoulder blades.

My hand traveled down from his stomach and under the waistband of his shorts and he breathed out pleasure, his throat croaky and bubbled with sleep. He couldn't turn without squashing me, so he reached his hand back and felt for the silk of the panties. His fingers played there for a while, toying with the fabric and me inside it; he was teasing, slow, enjoying the opiates of sleep and beer and sex, that drowsy indulgent line between wakefulness and sleep. I wriggled the silk panties down, pushing them with my feet towards the base of the bed.

"Baby," he murmured. "You just get back?"

"Mm-hmmm," I said softly, and I moved across so I could straddle him. And that was when he opened his eyes.

"What the . . . Jesus Christ!" With one arm he swiped me sideways, knocking me off him to Saskia's side of the bed.

"What the fuck are you doing here? Oh my God, oh my God, oh my God. You're insane!"

I pulled the comforter up over my belly and stared at him blankly. "I'm actually the opposite. If you'd just think clearly for a minute."

"Get out! Get fucking *out!*" he hissed as he ripped the blanket away from me.

Outside, a car pulled into the driveway, the music thudding as a passenger door swung open. From where I lay I could hear the tinkle of Saskia's voice and footsteps crunching on the gravel beneath the window.

"Oh, dear," I said. "Are you going to tell her or shall I?"

HP grabbed me by the wrist and flung me out of the bedroom, throwing my shirt at me before shutting the bedroom door. I could hear Saskia arriving, taking off her heels in the hallway. I rested against the spare room doorjamb, arms crossed against my naked rib cage. I let her pause at the sight of me, squinting into the shadowy hallway.

"What are you doing?"

"I'm sorry," I said, covering myself with my T-shirt. "It's a shame you had to find out this way."

She took two steps towards me. "Find out what?"

Before I could answer, their bedroom door flew open and HP blundered out, bare-chested in his boxers. He had both hands on his head. "Saskia, it's not what it looks like," he slurred.

I watched as she took in more details. My near nakedness. HP's disheveled hair.

She tottered, spindly and adrift down the hall, pushing past to inspect the bedroom. Then she turned to face HP, sinking down onto the edge of the bed.

"Saskia, it's not what you think," HP said. He rushed towards her. "She was in our bed. I thought it was you!" He sobbed the last word.

"Oh, for God's sake," I said, pushing forwards from my doorjamb, striding into their room. "You're not *that* drunk." HP covered his mouth with the cupped palm of one hand. Saskia's face went pale.

I wasn't ready. I wasn't ready for Saskia to spring up at me, all claws, kicks and spittle hissing. She pushed at my throat with her nasty little hands, her clenched fury knocking me off-balance, and I staggered sideways onto their carpet. "You want a fight, you fucking mole?" she whispered, her knees pressing me flat.

I wriggled but couldn't shift her.

"I will bring you down. Get out of my house and stay away from my family!"

She let go, pushing fury into my neck as she stood.

"Leave and don't come back," HP said. He took a half step towards me, as if he might jog over and kick me for a field goal. "Get in your car and go. Your game is over."

I went to the spare room, dressed, packed a few things into my suitcase and took off in my car for my mother's place.

chapter

21

Novak has completely lost his poker face.

"So, Angela . . ." He rubs his hand over his weak jawline. "Is that when you decided to get her back?"

"No, that was my last effort at breaking through to HP. I was done."

He scratches his head, leafing through his file. He's looking for something, anything, to keep me here.

"Can I go?" It's time: we've reached the finish. And now that the moment has arrived, it seems almost anticlimactic. I was half hoping he'd go up a gear and at least present something of a challenge.

He stands up and puts his hands in his pockets. "You're kind of a bad person, Angela. Has that occurred to you? You're driven by hate. That kind of toxicity can really eat a person up, compelling them to do nasty things."

My laugh is dry. "Okay. Can I go?"

Novak leans against the door. It's the cat and the mouse all over again. "You have one major problem, as I see it."

"You've got nothing on me."

"DNA of the missing woman found in your bedroom. Her favorite necklace tucked away in your book."

"I didn't put it there. Olive wanted me to have it."

"That's going to be hard for you to prove. I have to agree with Mr. Parker when he says your game is over."

"Arrest me then, Detective Novak." I lean back so that the chair tips. "In the meantime, where's my lawyer? I'm not saying anything more until you get me one."

And then he surprises me. He leaves and returns with a policeman, the man who deposited the plated macaroni late last night. The officer's cheeks are flushed.

"We have sufficient evidence to suggest you're involved in the disappearance of Saskia Joanne Parker," Novak announces, his voice churchy and too loud. "You're officially being held for longer. You've requested an attorney and one will be provided to you. Do you have any questions?"

I tilt my head and shrug.

"I'll take that as a no."

chapter

22

My attorney's name is Tate. I'm not clear if that's his first name or his last. He wears tennis shoes with his suit and has a new girlfriend, judging by the number of text messages he's already received in his first five minutes. He must be fresh out of law school because he's about my age; he's short-haired and overweight by thirty pounds, with a blond beard and a signet ring on his right pinkie.

I like him instantly. He sits next to me in the interview room while Novak is across from us with his file. Tate's cell beeps on the table, hopping it along a few inches.

"Ignore that," Tate says, but he doesn't make a move to switch it off.

"Can we pick up where we left off earlier?" Novak mutters, laying paper documents flat and resting his palms on top of them. He looks at Tate like locals look at tourists.

"Yep." He turns to me. "Are you ready?"

I nod.

"Angela," Novak begins. "We've established you have motive to cause the Parkers harm."

"Excuse me," cuts in Tate. "My client asserts she's caused *no harm* to any party. Leading the witness."

"We're not in court, Tate."

"No, but you can't put words in her mouth. Rephrase."

Novak blows out air into his cheeks. "We've established that your client wanted revenge on the Parkers for 'injustices' she felt they'd done to her. Is that fair?"

"She exacted her revenge when she attempted to have sex with Mr. Parker. Which, correct me if I'm wrong, Detective Novak, isn't a crime."

"But her hatred runs deeper. If she did that, then . . ."

Tate shrugs.

"Angela, did you try to insinuate yourself into the life of the Parkers, to possess everything they'd managed to build?"

"Don't answer that," Tate says.

"Didn't you long to become Saskia? That's pretty much what you've told me. Wasn't it eating you up? All those years and you couldn't oust her? When HP threw you out of the house, did you take it upon yourself to lure Saskia with a fake apology, with the express intention of causing her harm?"

"As your attorney, I strongly advise you not to answer that one, either."

"Angela, somebody coaxed Saskia to a secret location, and she went with full compliance. She organized a playdate for Olive, forgot to take her cell phone with her and didn't leave her husband a note. That to me suggests it was a meeting she was eager to attend."

"Is that a question?" asks Tate. "I'm struggling to hear it in among all the conjecture."

"Where is Saskia, Angela?"

"I've no idea," I say.

"You're still not upset." Novak smacks both hands on the table.

"Sure I am. I just don't like to parade my feelings for strangers. And I'm drained."

"That's right." Tate nods. "Two days of constant questioning can take a toll on a person's emotional thresholds."

Novak composes himself. "Where did you spend last weekend? June ninth and tenth?"

"Boston. With Mom. I already told you this."

"According to Freddy Montgomery's statement, you stayed with *him* at the Boston Hotel on Berkeley Street. Did you speak with Freddy Montgomery about your frustrations with the Parkers?"

"Probably. They had just kicked me out of their house." I glance at Tate.

"And was Mr. Montgomery sympathetic?"

"You'd have to ask him."

"Isn't it true that Mr. Montgomery would do anything for you?" Novak delivers the line for Tate's benefit; he's already tried that argument on me.

"I think he's my friend, if that's what you're asking."

"*Only* your friend, or are you sleeping with him? Is he part of your little manipulation game, too?"

"Objection," says Tate. "Irrelevant who my client sleeps with."

Novak rolls his eyes and mutters.

"Do you have anything else?" asks Tate. "Unless you have something new—like, say, *a body* with my client's DNA on it—I'm going to get my client out of here."

"Wait." Novak gets up and walks out the door.

Tate turns to me. "He's panicking."

"I know."

"Sit tight."

Tate takes a quick call, ending it with a happy sigh

as he slips his phone back into his pocket. "Sorry about that. Listen, like I say, we're talking hours now. I'd say two, max. Let's just stay a little longer, placate him, and soon you'll be home free—and you can carry on with your life."

I'm bored of this room and I'm bored of these people. Honestly, it seems to me that the only interesting humans in the world are the young ones. Year by year as we grow, a little more imagination rubs off us, like white paint from a fence. By adulthood, all we are is a horde of conditioned washed-out scarecrows, shuffling along with our heads full of hay.

I used to be nicer. When I was a kid, I never joined in with the neighborhood boys who pulled the legs off spiders. I never threw rocks at dogs. I held hands with all kinds of people and trotted alongside them, letting their faces beat down on me like a sun. I was a lot like Olive.

The way we live now, most people veil their

destructiveness and dress it up as love. They clothe it
and feed it and take it out on the town as their socially
acceptable form of devastation. They do as much damage as the next person.

All love stories are crime stories and all crime stories, love. If you say that's not true, you're not looking
properly. Perhaps when two people join, it's inevitable
the things they'll damage in each other. If that's what
Novak means by calling this a love story, then fine, I
totally agree with him.

Ezra fantasized about getting rid of his dog in high
school, but the truth is I've always had ways stacked up
in my head of how to clear my life of Saskia. But they
were thoughts, not actions, and you can't get in trouble
for thinking things. Because if you could, wouldn't everyone in the world be in jail?

Tate left the room a while ago to talk to Novak. Now
they come in together. Neither of them sits down.
Tate has no bag or pen with him and he's left his jacket
elsewhere, probably in the coffee room. Novak has a
glass jar crooked between his elbow and his left hip.
Tate's face is clammy with new stress.

"Are you letting me out?"

Tate shakes his head.

Novak stares into my face, his hooded eyes icicle-cold. "Look, Angela, here's your Manifestation Jar, as promised. Our forensic guys have delivered this back to us, and we've had a chance to read through it."

I look more closely at the mason jar as he stands it on the table. It's definitely mine. "I told you, anything I wrote in there is irrelevant, years old."

"What?" Novak cups his hand behind his ear. "Speak up."

I clear my throat and look at Tate. "It's just a bunch of dumb hippie voodoo. It was all my mother's idea."

"Was it?" Novak pulls latex gloves from an inside pocket of his suit, shaking his head. "I don't know why I bother with these things but, you know . . . You understand." He slips his long fingers into the gloves.

My heart's beating faster, and when I speak my tongue lisps. "Novak, you can't take anything that's in there seriously. It's not fair to dredge it up. I threw the whole jar out."

"Angela, let me do the talking," Tate says quietly.

The rubbery seal breaks. Novak rummages in to the elbow. The nerves in my fingers scream. "This is your handwriting, Angela?" He turns a piece of paper my way. "Good, just making sure." Novak unfolds the ragged sheet. "*HP loves me more.*" Novak tosses the note onto the table, where it quivers and shifts as I breathe. He goes in for a second dip. "*Her parents die in a car crash. She goes home to Australia and never comes back.*"

"Christ," says Tate as he readjusts his shirt at each armpit.

Novak pulls out a third. "*HP will come to his senses.*" He throws that one down into the pile. "I could go on and on. But you know what? I won't, because we already have more than we need."

"My client won't be talking further about this so-called exhibit. It's obsolete. Seven years beyond its sell-by date. Unsubmittable." Tate's chin is set.

Novak snorts laughter, getting ready to gloat, when the door to the interview room bursts open and the thickset policeman sticks his head in, his face ablaze.

"Sir, we need to speak."

Novak turns in his seat.

"You need to come."

Novak jumps up, collects the papers and clamps the jar back under his elbow, ramming his shin into his chair as he hurries.

"Wait!" I call. "Did they find her? Where?"

With Tate a few steps behind him, Novak pauses at the door, his fingertips on the door handle. He turns to face me. "Angela? Why aren't you asking if she's alive?"

chapter

24

It's the waiting that's the killer. I don't just mean in here, in this sterile little cube they've had me in for days, and I don't just mean for me. For everyone, it's the waiting that's the killer. Once you know what's coming for you, it's impossible to concentrate on anything else.

After I left HP that fateful Saturday night, I crept into my mother's house while she was asleep in her bed. I lay on the couch in the dark, staring at the silhouettes of trees as they moved in shadow on the ceiling. My neck hurt where Saskia had knelt on it.

I couldn't sleep. As the hours inched towards dawn, the feeling that I'd lost the most important piece of myself grew, until the panic was an oily sheen on my skin, slick and cold and unrelenting. When Mom found me at 7 a.m., I hadn't rolled over once.

"Goodness, did you sneak in here under cover of dark?" She leaned over the back of the couch, her hair smoother and less gray than it should have been. "How unsociable, darling."

She moved into the kitchen and began clanking coffee cups and pouring water. When the coffee sputtered to life, she returned.

"What's the matter with you, Angela?"

I hadn't been able to find any blankets in the night, and had resorted to the small starchy towel from the downstairs bathroom. It raked against my skin as I sat up.

"I had to leave the Parkers."

"Well, you'd expected to leave today anyway."

"I had to get out of there earlier than planned." I couldn't look at her. My stomach knotted inside me.

"Are you on bad terms?" She stared, hard and beady.

"Yes."

"With both of them, or just with her?"

My forehead creased, a signal I was about to crumble, and my throat burned to cry. Instead I managed a shrug.

"Darling." Mom came over to me, put a hand to my brow. "Whatever's happened, I'm sure it was way past due and will be for the best in the end. You've put all your eggs in that miserable Parker basket, and there was only so long before the basket tipped."

"I think I really lost HP."

Mom handed me a coffee. The heat of the mug was scalding to touch.

"I doubt that's true. Not really." She bunched me along the couch and sat down. The white flesh of her knee protruded from a gap in her housecoat. "You and HP have always been close. It's not like your father and me. When we fell out, it was like he'd dropped off the edge of the planet. And after years of marriage, no less. Believe me when I say you will get over this. And you'll be better for it when you do." She looked me over as she tucked the towel around me. "Perhaps I should tag along next weekend in Boston? In the meantime, we can be roomies this week! I can cook for two and we can drink gin together while we watch *Dancing with the Stars*. That'll lift your spirits, won't it, darling?"

Her words clattered off me like horseshoes thrown at an iron peg. I'd lost HP and I'd lost Olive. The couch was a pit and I was slipping in whole.

Later that morning I gave Freddy a call.

"They've banished me, Fred. I suppose it was only a matter of time."

"Good riddance to bad rubbish, I say. Are you all right? You sound down in the dumps."

"Freddy, am I a bad person?"

"What? Why on earth are you asking that?"

"Saskia and HP think I'm—"

"Oh, pish-posh. Who cares what they think? Listen, I'll see you for our mini break next Saturday. I've booked us a room at the Boston Hotel on Berkeley."

I sniffed. "My mother wants to come."

There was a long pause. "Really?"

I twirled the extension cord of the phone between my fingers. "She's missed me these past weeks and Cove is depressing."

He let out a small laugh. "Okay, fine, I'll make it a suite. We'll send her shopping on Saturday so that you and I will get some time." I heard him rap his knuckles on his desk. "Now, don't give HP or the Antipodean any more of your precious time. You are not a bad person, Angela Petitjean, you are gorgeous and underappreciated. It's time to assert yourself. Draw the line."

"You're the boss," I said, and hung up.

The following weekend, my mom and I flew to Boston. The Boston Hotel used to be a jail. It's a stone, gray behemoth, which in the right light could stand shoulder-to-shoulder with the grandeur of any building in Oxford. The original police station lanterns still flank the entranceway in bossy blue, and wherever you sit in the lobby you can look up at haunted ceilings and see the ghosts of old wrongdoing.

Freddy met us in the hotel bar, Precinct, on the Saturday afternoon. As Mom and I walked down the shiny stairs into the low-ceilinged bunker we found him sitting on a high stool by the bar, listening to the lilt of jazz on the sound system.

"Greetings!" He stood up from his stool and buttoned his blazer over a gleaming white shirt. "Welcome!

"How are you?" he asked me, taking my hand briefly. "There, there, you're with me now. You can forget all this awful business with those benighted ingrates. A better life begins right now." For the second that I hugged him, I felt safer than I had all week. "And Mrs. Petitjean, how glorious. You look younger every time I see you."

Mom fluttered a hand to her throat and blushed. She'd bought new shoes for the trip and swayed in them. Freddy just reached the height of her shoulders.

"Here, please, allow me . . ." He motioned us to a private table set back in a darker corner of the bar and pulled my mother's chair out for her. As she sat, he raised his eyebrows at me but couldn't maneuver over to the seat next to me. He was stuck by Mom. I suppressed a smile at our secret communication. "Ladies, I've taken the liberty of ordering us some cocktails." He gestured at the bartender with an upwards nod. "And I trust the room is to your liking?"

"It's huge, Freddy. You didn't have to treat us like royalty," I said.

Freddy bowed slightly. "It's my pleasure." He winked and raised his martini glass for a toast as we stretched our drinks forwards, green olives bobbling over the table at the bottom of our glasses. "Now, what news? Angela, my darling, I know you don't want to go into maudlin details, but seeing as Harrison Ford banished you from his house, you're very welcome to stay at mine."

"She won't need to," said Mom, sucking an olive off the stick in her drink. "She can live with me, and I can help her bring her life around."

"It's HP I want to bring around, Mom," I said. "Can we just leave it?"

A look of hurt passed over Mom's face, and I immediately regretted my tone.

"Sorry," I said. "Mom's been great, Freddy. We've been in a sorority all week, haven't we, Mom? I've learned endless things about ballroom dancing."

"It's been lovely, darling." She put down her olive stick carefully. "But honestly, I can help you set yourself straight, maybe even fix things for good with the Parkers—even if there was a bedroom incident."

"A bedroom incident?" Freddy's head tilted.

"Mom, that's private!" I'd tried hard to keep the facts of my dismissal from HP's house to myself, but in a weaker moment I'd let Mom in on it. Part of me needed help: I needed her to pull me out of the quicksand and tell me I hadn't ruined everything.

Freddy looked straight at me, like I was an old joke.

"You know what?" I pushed my drink away. "I don't really feel like parading my private life around for all to see, thank you, Mother. It's really none of your business. Nor is it yours." I tipped my chin upwards at Freddy.

"Absolutely. Absolutely right. Apologies," Freddy said.

"Yes, dear," Mom echoed. "You're right. I'm sorry. Your secrets are not mine to tell. Now let's just get past this and move on." She eyed Freddy meaningfully in a way I did not like.

The waiter drifted within waving distance, and Freddy took the opportunity to change the subject. "I'm a bit peckish. Would either of you ladies like a spot of food?" He pulled a menu from the center of the table and scanned the appetizers. I could see his brow creasing. "We could order here and have them bring it up to our room."

My mouth felt clammy. I was trying to get Freddy's attention, but he wouldn't look up from the menu. He flourished a hand at the waiter, who came over and took Freddy's orders for oysters and foie gras.

We went back up to our suite and ate on the silk couch, watching the sunset over the Charles River. I picked at my food, my headache thumping. Foie gras seemed wrong to me—a spread made from the choked, force-fed geese of France. I pictured them with hoses jammed down their throats, and felt guilty on their behalf. Had I been that pushy, that unkind? All of a sudden there was something horribly relatable about them.

The afternoon had blurred into evening; soon it would be time to go to bed.

"So where are you sleeping, Frederick?" Mom asked, pinching skin on the back of her hand and then pressing it flat.

"I'm not sure we've decided. But the master bedroom is that one . . ." He gestured to a set of closed white doors and strained to pop the cork out of a fresh bottle of Krug Brut Vintage. "Feel free to freshen up." He handed Mom her champagne.

"Oh, I'm perfectly fresh, thank you."

"Most likely I'll sleep on the couch," Freddy said after a pause. "You girls can take the bedrooms."

"That's fine," my mother breezed. "Whatever suits best."

Freddy sat down beside Mom and me as we watched the sun dip behind the embankment. Its globe glittered away to nothingness, leaving only scurrying people on the riverbank, oblivious to the insignificance of their lives. I don't know why, but I couldn't hold back my tears.

"Angela, good heavens, you're upset!" Freddy said, hunching low to get a good look at me. "What on earth's the matter?" He put his arm around my shoulders, and it spilled out of me then, my worst, deepest fear. I couldn't help it.

"I think there's something wrong with me."

He laughed as if I were making a joke.

"I think I might have something serious, like a personality disorder."

Freddy shifted deeper into the couch cushion, squashing me down. "Well, that's no biggie," he said. "Haven't we all."

"Angela, you're . . . fine. You're doing just fine," my mother said. "You were too involved, you know, too vulnerable, and Saskia was not protecting you. This too shall pass. Maybe now you can finally . . ."

"Move on?" Freddy offered.

"Yes," my mom said. "Freddy's absolutely right."

I paused, letting their words sink in. I looked from Freddy's face to Mom's, and what I saw there was new and unfamiliar. Their eyebrows arched with the same concern. Had they always had these expressions? Was it just that I'd never looked properly?

"I've been thinking the past few days about the

choices I've made lately, and . . . I'm scared. I don't know how else to put it." My nose ran and I wiped it with the back of my sleeve. Freddy pulled his handkerchief from the breast pocket of his blazer and passed it to me.

"Are you talking about sleeping with HP?" he said. "Because if you ask me, it's totally understandable. A mistake, for sure. But now you've got it out of your system."

"We didn't sleep together. He doesn't even want me. Probably never did. Oh, God, I'm such an idiot." I thought for a moment about the rich luxury of HP's sheets, the quiet of the house before it all went wrong. Pressure built at my temples like heat.

"You are not an idiot. You're my girl," Mom said, running a hand over my hair and tucking a strand behind my ear.

I thumped my thigh with a clenched fist. "I need it to stop. I can't live like this anymore—obsessed with all the wrong things. Why can't I be like everyone else, just living a normal life?"

Mom took my hand, even though it was damp with misery. "You're all worked up. You need to calm down."

"That's what I'm saying, Mom, there is no calm! I need help. I've got spiders in my brain and they won't stop crawling."

"Okay, let's not panic," Freddy said. "I mean, how many webs can a spider weave? Now you realize something new about yourself. So that's good. And . . . And I'm right here." He clasped me to him.

"You're not helping. It's not just about HP. It's about a family I found a place in." Freddy looked at my mother, and something passed between them that I couldn't quite catch. "It's about HP and Olive, being part of their lives. That's over now. Gone."

"I can see this is upsetting." Freddy tapped his forefinger to his lip. "How can we help sort this out for you?"

"I'm just a tragic sad sack, pining after someone who doesn't want me my whole life. It's turned me into something I'm not."

Mom shifted like the sofa was prickly. "Just try to be a bit kinder to yourself, darling," she said.

"I'm tired." I blew my nose loudly. "I'm tired of chasing the wrong things."

"You are being a little bit dramatic," Freddy said. "And very defeatist. You haven't turned into something you're not."

"Olive thinks I'm the witch in the story."

"Olive's five. She thinks monsters live under the bed," Mom said.

"But she's right. I've wanted to hurt Saskia. I've wanted her gone."

Freddy bit his lip. "I see," he said. "Perhaps when you get to that level, it might be considered a bit . . ."

"Obsessive," my mother said. "But, darling, I thought you'd gotten all your serious hate out years ago. Those manifestations you wrote, all that anger put into a jar . . ."

Freddy leaned in close to my neck, still holding his champagne glass. "Do you want me to have Saskia killed? I really don't like her, either. What a cow." He pressed the base of the flute against his knee so the crystal rotated, catching new light. "I've got all manner of contacts—all of them ex-military-contractor types."

"What, contract killers?"

"I could have her dead by tomorrow, around midday," he said. "Say the word—they'll send me her head in a fancy hatbox. I'll make a few calls on my hotline. Your mum can help out, right, take care of the sordid details?" He winked at Mom, then at me.

"Of course I could," Mom chimed. "Anything for my precious, exceptional daughter."

I rested my chin on my fist. "You'd really do that? For me?"

"My dear, I should have hired a sniper for their wedding," Freddy said, chuckling. Then he snapped his fingers in disappointment. "Bugger it, that was a chance missed."

Mom giggled at that.

"You could have hired me. I'd have done it for free," I said, and that got us all roaring. We laughed and laughed and laughed.

Freddy was the first to calm down. He refilled his glass and took a gulp. "Well, at least we've had a good chuckle. And we've solved one problem. Quite often with these things you have to name it to tame it."

Mom nodded. We sat quietly for a moment, everything turning somber again.

"You mustn't worry, sweetheart," Mom said. "We're here for you. We'll take care of everything. You leave it to us."

"We love you, Ange. We're both in your corner. And believe me, we're excellent people to have on your team."

When Tate comes back in, he hangs by the door and stares at me for a few seconds before he speaks. He takes off his tie and hangs it on the back of his chair.

"We're in trouble," he says.

I'm so tired I might cry.

"They pulled Saskia out of a lake an hour ago. Dead. That's the only thing they told me." Tate clears his throat. "I'm sorry to be the one to pass that on."

I can't get another clear thought, so I nod like I'm listening but my brain's sucking in on itself like mud in a geyser. Every time I inhale, the walls pull closer.

"Let's prepare ourselves now, Angela. Novak's coming for you, and we need to be ready."

I'm trying to steady my head, but I've been holding

back the truth. I haven't told a soul. It's sitting at every edge of me now, ready to spill out: all these hours in this room and I never said once that it was Freddy and Mom who came up with the plan.

"Angela, the only way to exorcise these demons of yours is to take them on full-force. Attack from the front. You need action." Freddy thumped one fist into the other. "You need to take charge."

The three of us were still sitting on that couch in Boston, watching the dying light.

"Let's wipe out this poisonous chapter," Mom added. "All it takes is letting go. We'll bury the past, start over and throw the entire book into the fire." Her eyes glittered. "Everything will be better after that."

"That's right," Freddy echoed, straightening his blazer. "Let the whole sorry thing go. Move on. Begin afresh. All of us." His sentences punched out like military coordinates. What was I to do but go along with it? Even talking about Saskia and the swirl she'd caused inside me was helpful—admitting to Freddy and Mom that my brain had grown crusty and unwell was like handing over a sickness to be cured. I was no longer alone in the labyrinth. I had allies. Whatever we did together would be our little secret.

Freddy organized every last detail, including contacting Saskia and inviting her to the lake to meet up with me. Thursday night was warm. Mom and I drove out to Elbow Lake in her car, the windows down as we sped along past the liquor store and north to the highway. There was heat left over from the day, like memory, beating upwards from the asphalt.

"Now, make sure you go through with it," she shouted over the *Les Misérables* CD she'd insisted on bringing, the woman's song strident and mournful. "Remember everything we've told you about fixing the problem once and for all."

I stretched my right hand out the open window, letting the air current push my flat palm up and down.

"All I'm going to do once I'm there is stand look-out, darling, just to make sure nothing goes wrong." She glanced sharply at the clock on the dash. "Freddy should be there by now, with Saskia."

We reached the track down to Elbow Lake, Mom's car bumping over the rutted grass to the shoreline. She parked fifty feet from the dock, and I could see Saskia standing alone down there, feathery and delicate in the evening sun. She was wearing a light-gray top that billowed behind her like a sail.

"How are we feeling?" Freddy strode towards Mom and me as we got out of the car and shut the doors. He was rubbing his hands together like we were about to eat a feast. "Angela? Are you up for this?"

My heart fluttered, mothy and condemned.

"In these situations"—he put his solid arm around

265

me—"it's best not to overthink it. Just get in there and do what has to be done."

"It's the only way to feel better and move on," Mom said, flanking me on the other side.

Freddy lifted his chin at Saskia. "She spoke all the way here about her need to resolve things. It's an entirely open door."

Saskia waved from the dock, her hand uncertain. I couldn't wave back. I yanked my neck out of Freddy's hug.

"I can't do this," I said.

"I think you'll find you can," said Freddy. "You'll never get a better chance than this one."

"You can end this, Angela," Mom said.

The two of them gripped my hands, walking me down to the dock. As we got nearer to Saskia, I could see her face, pale and strained but hopeful. After all this time, she still believed the world was a nice place. The wood of the dock was grainy, the nails rusted darker and deeper. I took two steps on the ramp while Mom and Freddy stood behind me on the last of the shore. When I turned back, they were waiting with their arms crossed.

"Go on." Mom flicked her fingers at me like this was normal, a necessary tearing-apart that parents ought to encourage. My mouth was dry as ashes. Saskia stood only ten feet from me, her thin arms wrapped around her ribs. Every now and then, she moved strands of golden hair from where the wind whipped them against her mouth. She didn't speak to me, but when she took a step towards me along the dock, I froze. Mom was wrong. I couldn't do this, it was insane.

I turned my back on Saskia and ran down the ramp onto the shore, past my mother and Freddy. I made it all the way to my mother's car before they caught up with me.

"What are you doing?" Freddy said, breathing hard. "This isn't the plan."

"I can't go through with it, Freddy. This isn't me." Overhead a bird cried out, shrieking and lonely, making me jump.

"You'll regret this later," Mom said, one arm propped against the side of the car. "You'll wish you'd been more proactive."

"No, Mom. I won't. I'm going home."

"Not in my car, you're not," Mom started, but Freddy put his hand on hers.

"Shelley, I think Angela's reached her limit. The best thing we can do now, as members of her team"—he paused for emphasis—"is to see this through *for* her."

Mom looked from Freddy to Saskia and back again. "What—us?"

"I think that's for the best. Let your daughter go home." He opened the driver's door of Mom's car and helped me into the seat. "Angela, you drive safely back to your mother's house. Don't worry about a thing. We'll explain everything to Saskia, won't we, Shelley?"

Mom nodded, although her neck muscles were taut. "We'll do what we have to do."

"Off you go now." Freddy slammed the door. "Everything will be fine after tonight." He smiled, but his teeth looked odd.

As I bumped my way back up the grass to the road, *Les Misérables* blaring, I saw Mom and Freddy walking down to the dock, talking close to each other's faces. Freddy now had his arm around Mom. The rearview mirror bounced their reflections wildly, but the last I saw of them both—of my mother and Freddy—was them stepping onto the ramp. Freddy's arms extended towards Saskia, and he was just about to reach her.

chapter

26

The clock is ticking past 5 p.m. Novak holds the door for someone, and with a jolt of relief I realize my mother is behind him. She flitters by the doorway, her movements bird-like and skittish. I clamber out of my chair and run to her, hug her tight.

"Mom," I say. "Are you all right?"

She opens her mouth to answer but nothing comes out, and when she looks at me her eyes are watery and moribund like the trout at the Saturday-morning city markets she used to take me to as a child. Hugging her is like holding a cold pole.

"Why?" Mom's voice barely registers enough sound to shape syllables. "Why did you do it?"

Mom sobs now, a sound like she might be drowning.

She drapes herself into the chair opposite Tate. I return to my seat, my arms limp by my sides, shock filling me.

No, no, no. This can't be happening.

Sitting down in the only other chair at the table, Novak places himself next to my mother. "Saskia Parker is dead." He watches me for a reaction. I give none. Across the table, Mom's breaths are swift and rickety, and then she collapses, crying into her hands.

Is she for real? Why is she doing this to me?

"We have of course notified her next of kin." Novak's words sound automated: he's studying more than he's speaking. "You don't seem surprised to hear of her death, Angela."

I can't tell what's inside my head and what's outside of it. Everything's radio fuzz. Why isn't Mom yelling at him, defending me? How can she do this?

"Do you know what happens to a body that's been submerged in water for close to forty-eight hours? Can you picture it? We thought perhaps you'd like to tell your mother what you did. Hence the family reunion."

Mom looks up, her eyes drilling into mine.

"Mom," I say, "why are you looking at me like that? Say something!"

"How, Angela? How could you?" she asks. "How?" And then it's more tears.

Novak steps in. "According to your mother's

270

statement, you very recently referred to yourself as 'having become something you are not' and said there were 'spiders' on the inside of your head. Is that true?"

"Upon advice from her counsel, my client will not be speaking further to this matter." Tate puts his hand on my knee.

"Oh, it's not just Mrs. Petitjean who references your client's diseased state of mind." Novak's oily with his own cleverness. "I have another signed statement here that corroborates everything Mrs. Petitjean has said." He reaches inside his suit pocket and pulls out a white sheet. It's been folded neatly, like someone's run a thumbnail down the crease.

"This is the signed statement from Freddy Montgomery, made earlier this morning. Shall we have a read?" Novak unfolds the paper, pressing it flat on the table. "*Angela Petitjean, her mother and I shared a bottle of champagne in my hotel suite in Boston. At the time she was troubled by what she termed a 'personality disorder' and also openly admitted that she wanted to hurt Saskia. She said she 'wanted her gone.' I'm afraid I distinctly remember the phrasing.*"

I half swallow, looking from Mom to the letter and back. After everything we'd gone through together? "No!" I shout. "That's not fair! Did he tell you he offered to kill Saskia himself? He said he knew contract

271

killers who could send him her head in a box! Mom, tell them!"

"Oh, Angela, I tried to help you," Mom says, her face cleaving into sobs once more. It's a master performance, the likes of which I've never seen before.

Novak folds up Freddy's paper. He's barely able to contain his utter dislike of me. How can I prove what they did? How?

It's like the room has tipped and everything's sliding. I can't get a proper grip.

"Of course it was Elbow Lake," Mom says suddenly, her jaw jerky and sour as she spits out the words.

"I'm sorry?" Tate says.

"That's where they found Saskia's body. Elbow Lake. It's where my daughter first loved HP." My mother heaves and crumples. When she finds the stamina to sit up again, she finally looks right at me and there are layers upon layers in her eyes, like filters in front of a lens. Fear is a layer and pain is in there, too, but the thickest of them all is guilt.

Tate turns to me, wide-eyed. My throat constricts and I'm shaking. "We went there for grad, HP and me." I think of us on the dock, eighteen years old, HP standing on the edge in his board shorts with his back to that clear water. *You walk around with your eyes closed, too.*

"I'm so sorry, sweetheart." Mom wraps her arms

around herself. "But I can't in good faith protect you any longer."

I try to think of a single time in my life when I felt protected by her. Never. Not once.

"We're charging you with first-degree murder and obstruction of justice." Novak gathers up his paperwork, threading Freddy's statement back into his pocket. "Within the hour it'll be official." He helps Mom out of her chair and she walks with him to the door, her legs stalky as if they won't bend properly.

Once they're gone, Tate exhales noisily. "Do you have any idea what the hell's going on here?"

"It wasn't me, Tate. I know it looks like it was, and everything's stacked up against me, but I swear to God, I never killed Saskia. I walked away." I rub my nose against the knuckles of my thumbs. "There were times when I thought about it; but when I said those words to Freddy, it was me trying to rid myself of the compulsion. And then, suddenly, Freddy and my own mother were hatching a plan, pushing me to it. They even got Saskia, brought her to Elbow Lake, Tate. I could have hurt her but I didn't, because we don't all act on our worst intentions, do we?"

Tate scratches his beard, distracted. When he speaks, it's a throwaway comment, an aside. "If we did, there wouldn't be enough rooms like this one."

I want to hug him. He nods and stands, his hands in his pockets. "If you didn't do this, Angela, how are we supposed to show that they did?"

I close my eyes. "I don't know," I say. The darkness feels good.

chapter

27

When I was a kid, my parents took me on a road trip to the West Coast and we drove right through the middle of a tree in Northern California. It was an old tree, knotted and stoic from the side view, but minivans were rolling right through the middle of it while kids hung out the windows scraping their Slurpee cups along the ridges of the tree's callused innards. I could hear their plastic straws rattling like sticks down a washboard. Mom turned from the passenger seat to explain that the giant sequoia was rotting from the inside out. At the time I didn't realize the extent to which she was doing exactly the same thing.

She was so focused on my life being different from hers. Throughout her marriage to Dad, the years dripped by for her in humdrum mundanity as she traveled further and further away from exceptional, becoming little more than a mediocre housewife. Long lost were the days of her glamorous youth. After a few years with Dad, nobody noticed her. For twenty-five years my dad studied Greek while my mom chopped vegetables, and if I think about it now, I get why she was so desperate for me to do something with the chances I had. *Claim your life*, she told me at every opportunity, *before somebody claims it for you*. I wonder now if I ever really understood what she was saying. I always thought she was talking about HP.

After I shared the details of what had happened with HP, my mother ran with the drama. She ranted about what I must do next, how I must get my life in order now, show them all up. *Finish it, darling, drive it home*. Leaving things as they were was *lily-livered*—what I needed was *closure*. How carefully she hid her own devastations. She hid her meanings, too, never outright saying what she thought I should do, but lining every sentence with suggestion, like silk behind a curtain. The more we talked, the more insistent she became.

It was her idea for me to invite Saskia to the lake—hers! And Freddy supported it wholeheartedly.

"Elbow Lake is the perfect setting," she'd said. "It's so symbolic. Everything began there and now you can finish it there. I love a full circle."

"What if I don't want to meet with her? What if I never want to see her again?"

"Forgive and forget." It had become her mantra, delivered by rote so many times that I think even she had lost track of what she was asking.

Freddy, for his part, must surely have been trying to help me when they first thought up the plan. If my mother's intentions always had a slant of self-interest—some kind of vindication—his were always true. But here, now, with Novak closing in, he's reverted to his Machiavellian self: Freddy the businessman, vise-like in a pinch. He might have been acting on my behalf at Elbow Lake, but the statement he's written today is a sellout, nothing more than a wriggle of desperation. He knows I can't prove him a liar and I'll never forgive him for it, or forget.

And beneath everything piled up on top of me, big-eyed and quiet in the wreckage, is Olive. Her sweetness when I slept next to her; the way she tried so hard to give me her mother's necklace as a gift. Only she really noticed how sad I was, what I needed most. And I'll never be allowed to see her again.

chapter
28

Novak returns to the room alone. He sits down in his chair without speaking, staring across the table at Tate and me as he readjusts the chain of his pocket watch and primps the cuff links in his sleeves.

"Anything else?" he says after a long silence. He's roostered and smug with triumph.

"You've got it wrong," Tate tells him. "Your case isn't as watertight as you'd like to believe."

"See you in court, Tate." He stands. "It's over, Ms. Petitjean. Our story has its ending."

My eyes feel raw and puffy.

"You've talked a lot about the years you've spent with Mr. Parker; God knows we're all aware it's the greatest love affair of the century. But I have to say we've gotten to know each other well in the past couple of days. Haven't we? Perhaps we can be pen pals? You can send me postcards from jail." He straightens, buttoning the front of his jacket, and doesn't look back as he walks away.

After a few seconds, Tate stands and lifts the strap of his bag over his head and around his chest like a bike courier. He moves near the door and puts his hands in his pockets.

"I really hate that guy." He shrugs. "Look, I have to get going here. Let's try and stay positive. Eat the food they bring you. Stay hydrated. Whatever happened today and whatever Novak thinks, it's not the end of the story, so no dark thoughts, okay?"

I put my chin on the table, and my eyes feel heavy as they brim with tears.

"It'll be my word against Mom's."

"Yep. Hers and Freddy Montgomery's." He sucks the hair beneath his lower lip. "I don't know what else to tell you. Are you scared?"

"I don't know what I am."

My heart feels listless, as if inside my chest there's a drummer who's had enough of the beat.

"I'm gonna go now. It'll be okay," he says, then ambles out.

Soon they'll take me out of this room and put me into an even smaller one. I wonder if it'll have a window. Shards of late-afternoon amber light spear in from outside, cutting the wall into pieces.

Everything in my life is gone now but sadness. Perhaps that's all I've ever really had for company. Mom, HP, Freddy, Dad, even Ezra—they all abandoned me one way or another. I've become a ghost story that HP will whisper to himself in the dark. I wonder what he will tell Olive about me, in the future. The steps the two of them take in daylight won't ever be quite as certain, and I never would have wished that for them. It's not what I pictured at all. This whole thing began in loneliness and it wasn't meant to end in it. Oh, Saskia. The universe came for her just as I said it would, but nobody listened to my warnings. But there's irony at every turn, because here we are at the very end, and Saskia's still taking everything I have.

THE URGE TO DESTROY IS CREATIVE. If only they would shine their flashlight at the actual monster. Everyone in this building has me pegged as the psychopath, the one who destroyed the lives of others. Don't they know that everybody has the urge to destroy? It's simply a sliding scale. Put a crowd of a hundred people in a room and wait. Eventually the psychopaths will emerge, and I'm telling you now, they won't be who you first suspected and there'll always be more than one. Watch the successful people who push to the front; keep an eye on the hierarchy as it establishes itself. Take Freddy, for example: if I'm a psychopath, then so is he, so is Mom, and do you really think Novak isn't? Deep inside the fibers of everyone's brain, where the real stories are told, there's always dark intent. And Novak said it himself—he wants me in jail, he wants to see me suffer.

But they've grappled me into a box now and they'll spend the remainder of my time here hoping the lid stays on tight. It's okay. I know how they feel. I've been battling demons for so long. No one wants to see the truth: wrong, right, guilty, innocent, honest, dishonest; with the right set of circumstances, we're all capable of anything.

Just as I'm scraping at the rusted window clasp, scrabbling fingerprints down the glass of the pane, Novak pushes the door open.

"We're moving you." He bends back out of the doorway to nod at someone down the hall and give them a thumbs-up. Then he ducks back in. "What did you just say?"

"I didn't speak."

"Uh, yes you did."

"Do you know anything about loneliness, Detective Novak?"

"That's enough. Let's go."

A man in a gray suit passes by and Novak backs

out into the corridor again, wedging his shiny shoe into the gap of the doorjamb. I hear the deep pitch of their voices, the lilt of it low, like mooing. Above the door, the video camera continues to log every move I make. Who's on the other side of that machine? Forty or so hours of my life captured on tape. I stand still with my face turned up to the lens.

Tate says there's hope yet; he says it like we're winners. What he doesn't understand, though, is how steadily people decay. We all look the same on the outside while sadness eats at our core. Dad, HP, Ezra, Mom, Freddy—even Olive—there's absence tunneling out of each of them. Freddy will walk free—he'll have the best lawyers money can buy. He won't contact me again. Mom will creep around Cove in her silk scarf and claim no knowledge whatsoever of any wrongdoing. If the forensics team actually does their job, maybe they'll find her DNA on Saskia. Maybe they'll see that more than one person killed her. Mom will spit all the way to jail, trying with every step to take me there with her. If it comes to it and she's incarcerated, she'll find some way to create a prison hierarchy, placing herself on top of the rancid peak.

Tate will stick with me. He'll look me dead in the eye, perhaps because he's at home on the road of loss. Maybe there's something still to be learned from him.

Buck up! he'll say, as the days sag towards the trial. *You never know what might happen!* But that's the problem: I know exactly what the world can do to a person.

I miss Olive. There's a certainty in children, a belief that gets lost in adults. Tell a kid there's a monster in the bathroom and they'll ask you what color it is. They accept everything and it makes them powerful, not vulnerable. We should elevate our children's capacity to believe things. Olive Parker, stay pristine: don't grow up at the mercy of anything, especially false optimism. I'll write you letters you'll never read. I'm your godmother, don't forget! Your mother turned me into that, too.

Novak steps back into the room, holding the door open with his foot. "Let's go," he says again. "It's time."

He leads me out into a corridor where the air is cooler. The walls are painted yellow and covered in posters with faces I'd like to spend more time studying. We move quietly along, leaving my fetid room behind.

Novak thinks he's won and I'm defeated, but the truth is I let something go in that space—all that frantic want, all the obsessiveness—it's like I've talked away a grand tapestry of wrongs. The farther I move now from the interview room, the more the dark thread unravels. I loved one person my whole life, and while everyone else postured and jigged and reefed their feelings into hostility, here I am emerging with that love intact. I may carry all of the blame, but I still have the memory of true happiness.

I didn't hurt anybody, not really, not the real kind of hurt. The tapestry of my sins is small. Can't you see the filament, Novak, looping heavy along the corridor as it comes undone? Let it unwind, let it unspool around me, because wherever we're going, Novak, whatever dark little hole you put me in, I'll close my eyes and know that I'm free. The spiders aren't crawling anymore.

chapter
29

It was warm as we drove out to Elbow Lake. A warm night, full of the leftover heat of the day. Mom's CD blared as she spoke to me of peace, of letting toxicity go, all the ways I could forgive and forget.

At the bottom of the bumpy, tufted hill, Saskia was already sitting on the dock. We parked and Freddy greeted us, his face flushed with possible absolution. He rubbed his hands together as if it were cold. "I know it's not your top choice, but you'll feel so much better once you've spoken with her. At times like this, Angie, it's important to just do what needs to be done."

Near the shoreline, the mud was wet underfoot. Saskia's shirt billowed out behind her, her frame thin and vulnerable. She wasn't wearing shoes.

She waved from our dock—an uncertain wave, but there was still hope in her fingers as they trailed the air.

"Off you go, dear." Mom released me towards the water like a dove. "Do everything we told you. Say all the words we've practiced, and it'll all be fine. You'll be amazed how easily you can let go once you've properly apologized." She nodded with her eyebrows raised. How proud she would be of me if only I'd do this one thing.

I walked past the char of the old stone fire pit, blackened with fires of grads I no longer knew, and crossed the slats as they stretched out over the water. My legs were stiff, my joints rigid. Rusted nails jagged out of the wood, the grain fibrous and mealy and damp.

"Thanks for coming. I was hoping you would," I said, and she shook her head, her eyes so giving, so trusting, so evolved. She held a pebble in her cupped palm, rolling it around against her loveline and lifeline. She looked at me then, almost apologetic, almost contrite. I didn't move closer.

"Freddy said you wanted to chat," she said.

"That's right. More or less." I turned to see Mom and Freddy leaving, my mother's arm threaded through his. They walked back up the hill to Freddy's car and both got in. How sure they were of the power of forgiving and forgetting. Saskia and I watched the car creep up the bumpy ground and then gather speed as it found the road and was gone. I took a deep breath and turned back to Saskia.

"I'm trying to get over what you did," she said.

"Can you?" I asked. HP had skimmed stones, bare-chested, beautiful, exactly where she stood.

"I'd like to think we can be bigger people. Both of us," she said. She whipped her pebble into the lake. By her ankle was a thick, heavy rock, sharp and fated and waiting.

With her back to me, she didn't even realize I'd picked it up.

acknowledgments

Thanks to Nita Pronovost and Sarah St. Pierre for eventually managing to get me to the right picnic, and for all the fun along the way. Thanks to Liz Whitehead, whose concept of what the front cover should look like was quite brilliant. And to my agent, Carolyn Forde, who's tireless and amazing and with whom I'll one day tour Europe. I also need to thank Almeda Glenn Miller and Adrian Barnes for their inspiring classes at Selkirk College: they lit a fire under me, and here we are. Kristen Webb helped me with early ideas for nasty things characters could do; Kate Walker was my chapter-by-chapter reader, cheering me on; and Linda L. Richards gave me a great first edit. Tracey Mozel is my constant tech support, and I owe her much more than the Leo's Greek Pizza and red wine with which I repay her. Thanks, also, to Jo Lyle in Sydney, who reminded me of how Australians form sentences when I got rusty after a nine-year gap.

293

ACKNOWLEDGMENTS

To Robbie and her clan in Canada and my family in England—Jonathan and Sue Watt, Jo and Sal—thanks for all the love and reinforcement, and may you never read any of the rude scenes. And finally, most of all, thanks to Clint, Cash and Ruby. It's really all for you. Everything is. Thanks for not waking up when I tiptoed past your doors at 5 a.m. to write in a quiet house.

OUR LITTLE SECRET

ROZ NAY

A Reading Group Guide

for discussion

1. When Angela first meets Detective Novak, he asks that she fill in the blanks about Saskia. In order to answer Novak's questions, Angela goes back ten years, despite the fact that she doesn't meet Saskia until after high school. Why does Angela choose to begin her story from this point?

2. In the interrogation room, Angela notices a small line of graffiti on the wall: THE URGE TO DESTROY IS CREATIVE. When reading the novel, did these lines affect your interpretation of Angela or the stories she was telling?

3. During the course of the book, both Angela's and HP's names change according to who is addressing them. She is Angela, Little John, or LJ; he is HP or Hamish. What do these nicknames indicate about the characters and how they relate to themselves and others?

4. Discuss Angela's relationship with HP. They started out as best friends, and then they started dating. How did you feel when they got together? Why do you think they broke up?

5. In high school, HP says that Angela is his soul mate, but Saskia believes she and HP are soul mates. Do you think that HP and Angela were meant to be? Can you have more than one soul mate?

6. When HP first befriends Angela, he tells her, "Some secrets you have to earn." Does Angela

earn HP's secrets? If yes, how? How does Detective Novak earn Angela's secrets?

7. What were your initial impressions of Freddy? As Angela's friend, do you think he had good intentions? Was he a good or bad influence in Angela's life?

8. Angela's dad was determined to get her into an Ivy League school, and her mom was obsessed with Angela dating HP. Why do you think her parents were fixated on these life goals? Did these pressures affect Angela even after she finished high school? How so?

9. Angela's mom suggests that Angela make a Manifestation Jar in hopes that she can forgive and forget after her miserable summer watching HP and Saskia together. But when the jar resurfaces, Detective Novak uses it as evidence against Angela. Do you think Angela believed her manifestations would come true? Did the jar have a positive or negative affect on her life?

10. People often have a time in their life that they think of as golden, or as the best time of their

life—for Angela, that time is high school and her relationship with HP. How does this idolization of her past affect her present and future?

11. Saskia is obsessed with elephants because they mate for life and mourn their dead. Why is the elephant such an important symbol? And what is the significance of the necklace that Detective Novak presents to Angela?

12. Later in the novel, Saskia tells Angela, "Sometimes I think we met on the same night because of fate." Do you think Angela believes in fate? Does fate direct Angela's actions? How?

13. Is Angela a trustworthy narrator? Why or why not?

14. Discuss the structure of the book. What effect does alternating between Angela's present interrogation and her memory of the past have on the story? Did learning about Angela's past help you better understand her future actions?

15. Is Angela a sympathetic protagonist? Did your feelings about Angela change as you read the book? If so, how?

16. Discuss the power of love in the novel. Discuss the power of obsession.

17. How does the author foreshadow the final events of the novel? Did you see the twist coming or were you surprised by the novel's outcome?

18. Could Saskia's death have been prevented? Why or why not?

19. Discuss Angela's final revelation to Detective Novak. Is she manipulating him or does she truly believe in her own version of the events?

20. What do you think happens to the characters after the novel is over? How do you think the events will impact each of their lives and relationships going forward?

a conversation
with Roz Nay

This is your debut novel. How long has this story been with you, and what is your writing process like? Did the story change and take shape as you went along?

The novel began as a one-thousand-word story I wrote in a creative writing class a few years ago. After I'd written it, Angela's voice stayed with me: I knew she had more to say, and that writing it from her point of view would be fun on a grander scale. I wrote the novel in a year; I tend to go like an Energizer Bunny until I reach the safety of a third draft. The shape of the story definitely changed as it went. Early drafts saw Angela stealing Olive, which was the most despicable thing I could have Angela do at the time, since Olive is very closely modeled on my own daughter. Through edits, both the crime and the victim changed. Secretly I was relieved—I could then stop hugging my daughter so maniacally.

Why did you choose to tell the story from the inside of an interrogation room?

The interrogation room came naturally: I liked the enclosed space of it, the idea of writing an entire story that, in the present sense, really doesn't move scene. I also enjoyed the dynamic of Novak and Angela; when you only have two people in a room, you can have all kinds of fun with how they evolve together.

The love story between Angela and HP is so captivating and endearing but is part of something much larger and darker. Did your imagining of the book always involve both a compelling love story and a mystery, or did one come before the other?

I always wanted to write a high school–era romance, because there's a poignancy to those years—a tenderness—and I wanted to get that onto paper somehow. Of course, it's much more interesting to mix tenderness with creepiness. I wanted the whole book to be ambiguous in those ways—is the love story sweet or is it dangerous? Is Angela relatable or is she psychotic? Are all of the characters likeable or badly behaved? I always wanted everything to be a bit of both.

Have you ever made a Manifestation Jar? What would you write for it?

I haven't made a Manifestation Jar, but I have been wishing hard on eyelashes for decades. Is that the same thing? I live in a town where manifestation is all the rage. If I were to put scraps of paper into a jar, most of them would have "Publish a novel" on them, so perhaps there's something to it . . .

Angela seems to be stuck in the memory of her high school experience. Is there a time in your life that you idealize or remember with great fondness?

Yes! Of course! I think everyone's nostalgic for those brightly colored years of youth and young adulthood, where you have twenty friends at all times and everything's just about to be fun. I can relate to Angela wanting that brightness back, but luckily I've evolved more healthily than she has so I'm not harboring anything damaging.

What books or films influenced you while writing this novel?

I read a lot of psychological thrillers, and writers like Harriet Lane, Jessica Knoll, and Emma Cline inform everything I'm learning. As a just-forming teenager, I read *The Collector* by John Fowles, a book that really rattled me. It's a master class in how to write an eerie, obsessive, first-person narrative, where readers are given only the psychopath's point of view. I think Fowles's book influenced *Our Little Secret* more than I realized as I was writing it. For

TV shows, I watch *Luther* and other British crime dramas, and I noticed the interrogation room aspect of *The Affair*, which struck me as similar in terms of whose version of events to trust.

Are there any real-life events or people that inspired the book? You've spent time in Britain, Australia, and the U.S. Are Freddy or Saskia based on people you met in their respective countries?

I think writers are thieves and store aspects of a whole cast of characters they know or observe. All the characters in the book are slivers of different people I've noticed, but mostly they're all slivers of me. I stole the voice of Freddy from a guy I spoke to briefly at a Christmas party in London about twenty years ago. It's surprising the things writers stash. HP's based largely on my husband, which he'll like me saying, because HP comes out of the whole thing quite well. I keep telling my husband that HP's better-looking, but he's not having it.

Which character did you identify with most, and why?

I'm laid-back like HP, I'm idealistic like Saskia, I'm snobby about stupid things like Freddy, I'm secretly dark and fearful like Angela. I'm all of them. But mostly I'm Angela. Except I wouldn't hit anyone on the head with a rock, or haven't yet.

about the author

© Lisa Seyfried Photography

ROZ NAY's debut novel, *Our Little Secret*, was a national bestseller, won the Douglas Kennedy Prize for best foreign thriller in France, and was nominated for the Kobo Emerging Writer Prize for Mystery and the Arthur Ellis Best First Crime Novel Award. Roz has lived and worked in Africa, Australia, the U.S., and the UK. She now lives in British Columbia, Canada, with her husband and two children.

RozNay.com
@RozNay1

**Turn the page for a
sneak peek of**

**Coming to bookstores
Summer 2020**

The woman holds the baby close and ghost-dances by the window. She can see her reflection in the glass. She doesn't mind being awake with her little boy at this odd, witchy hour when everyone else is asleep. This moment is a secret that only they share.

He is olive-skinned, familiar, although a far cry from her own pale coloring. *It doesn't matter*, she thinks. *He's mine and I'm keeping him.*

Outside, the street is quiet. The mountains in the distance watch over the sleeping town. She concentrates on the cowrie-shell curl of his hand. His fingernails are tiny and perfect, little crescent moons in each one. Did she make those? In one of his hands is a worn old clothespin that he's been gripping for days.

A dog's bark pierces the silence, and the baby startles and throws out his arms. *How powerful babies are*, she thinks. *How vulnerable.* She lifts her shirt and juggles him until he finds her breast. They fit perfectly together; they're made for each other.

A few moments later, the baby unlatches, frustrated, and she prods at his lips, her brow darkening.

"I'm sorry," she says to him. "Shhhh." He doesn't even try to latch again. Instead he fusses and turns his head away.

"Hey," she says, her voice louder. "It's just us now. You'll never see her again." The baby blinks, working up to a cry, and they stare at each other for a second, old souls reconnected, like there was never any loss before and nothing ever went wrong.

"You're okay, little one, you're safe now. There, that's better."

In a minute, she'll fetch him formula from the fridge, warm it up, test the temperature of it against the tender flesh of her inner arm. She knows how to do all of this: She's a natural. Finally everything is exactly as it should be.

alexandra

In the dream I am running and my sister is behind me. The ground is brittle, hard against my summer feet, and as with every dream, I think I'm rushing to save something, to stop it, but it's not that. It's so much worse. I can hear Ruth gaining on me—she's bigger than me—and she grazes the back of my shirt with her fingertips as I strain to run faster. When she finally grabs me, as she always does, she pulls me down into the dust and her sharp fingernails dig into the little-girl flesh of my arms. *It's just a game!* I scream, *We're only playing!* and I jolt upright in bed, my feet pedaling at the sheets, my tongue pasted against the soil of my mouth.

I lie panting for a minute. I thought the dreams would lessen but they're getting worse. They're always of her, or the version of her I last saw all those years ago. It's crazy to be so afraid of her; I don't even know where she is.

I tiptoe out of bed, careful not to wake up Chase, and stumble to the kitchen to get water, to put out this fire in my head. I'm so thirsty all the time. By the sink, I run cold, clear water and drink from the tap, splashing a little to my forehead.

Chase's loft is high-ceilinged and open concept, a one-bedroom that's short on doors and boundaries. Some couples might find that claustrophobic, but I don't. I find it companionable. I can just see him from where I stand by the sink: He's a muscular guy, but he breathes so softly, his tanned arm lolling against the crisp white sheets. I've no concept of where he goes when he sleeps, but it's an opposite dreamscape to mine.

Outside the sky is trying for an early blue. It's June but there's still a seven a.m. gray that leaks slowly into color. In this Colorado town, we're never too far from the creep of the glacier, a silent advance I can't help but find sinister. Chase, though, he loves everything about the mountains. On my way to the walk-in closet, I trail a fingertip across the tall canvas print of him by the front door, a professional mountain shot of his body upside down, hucking a twenty-foot drop on skis. I could never do that, wouldn't even know where to begin. But he's good in environments that I'd find daunting. He rarely ponders such things as his own mortality. Behind him, snow wisps delicately to eclipse the sun. I have to admit it's a beautiful photo.

Once I've pulled on skinny jeans and a T-shirt that isn't too crumpled, I grapple my hair into a topknot and grab my khaki jacket and my old leather satchel. I lift the satchel over my head so the strap lies diagonal across the front of me. My Vans are by the front door and I kick my feet into them, wondering if at twenty-five it might be time to buy shoes that aren't best suited to the average fourteen-year-old boy. But my job doesn't require a corporate dress code. As a Child Protection social worker, it's best if I look relatable.

Tucked away in the Rocky Mountains, Moses River is isolated in the winter months, but now the trees along the sidewalk are in bloom, the buds bulging with optimism. Locals mill about on Main Street, coffee in tall travel cups as they lean against their parked trucks. Wheels of mountain bikes hook over every tailgate—if there's bustle it isn't work-related. LIFE IS BEAUTIFUL reads more than one bumper sticker. But ask any social worker in this town and they'll tell you life around here is a lot of things, not all of them beautiful. But we're trying. We're trying for the kids who don't believe the bumper stickers, for the kids who live the truth.

As I walk up Main, I think about Minerva's email

from last night. It was hassled and hurried as usual, but she told me there was a report of negligence involving a little boy and his parents, a couple called the Floyds. I haven't heard the name before but from the tone of the email, it seemed like she was familiar with them. If she wants me on board, the case must be an ugly one. It always is when there's a baby involved. A little baby boy.

Minerva Cummins used to work in Mental Health and Addictions before she crossed over to Family Services, and she's never shaken it off. Every exchange I have with her feels like she's trying to help me out of some kind of saddening entrenchment. Even as I'm solving problems, she'll sigh with her eyes closed as if I'm the cause of them. Sometimes I wonder if that's why her husband divorced her. My boss, Morris, rarely puts me and Minerva together on cases—perhaps because he knows that as one of the older, more experienced social workers on the team, she can be patronizing. *She's a mother, Alex,* Morris told me once in his office. *But don't let her mother you.*

An unexpected cold blast of air hits me as I round the corner onto Cedar Street, and I jog the next few steps to the Lovin' Oven bakery. The bell above the robin's-egg blue door jingles as I enter and I'm greeted by the smell of butter tarts. The bakery is compact, with one long counter, various chalkboards on brick with the handwritten names of soups, rows of golden-fresh bread stacked on shelves behind the till, and three rough wooden tables for eating at, all of them rectangular with benches. I do a quick scan of the room as I enter. Minerva's not here yet. For all the dedication she claims to have, it's rare that she arrives on time to anything.

Once I've bought a coffee, I find a seat at the far end of the long table and wait for her. Over in the corner, two old ladies in matching knitted hats share a pot of tea. For a second, I wonder if they're sisters. The thought stops my breath.

But then the bell above the door jingles and Minerva strides toward me, corduroy pants chafing noisily as she moves. Her brown bob is still wet from the shower. It looks plastic, like hair you press onto Lego people.

She stops in front of me at the opposite bench. "Another day, another dollar."

"Morning," I say. "Are you ready to go?" I half-stand.

"Chill your boots! I need to brief you first, and you know I can't do anything without a strong coffee."

Coffee is why she wanted to meet early? I reluctantly sit back down while Minerva orders her coffee then settles into a seat as though we have all the time in the world—all the time in the world when a young child's well-being is at stake.

"So," I say, careful to hide my impatience. "Tell me about this baby boy and his parents."

"Frank and Evelyn Floyd have a history of drugs and alcohol addiction." She takes a wary first sip of her drink. "Basically, they were druggies, troublemakers before they had a child. But they've been better since he was born."

"Okay. . . . So then why are we both going on this visit?" I ask. What I really want to say is get a move on.

"The baby's name is Buster," she says, dodging my question. She pauses, relishing the Floyd baby's name, hoping I'll laugh at it, but I don't. "Earlier this week, they left him outside in the car while they went into the post office. Some Good Samaritan called it in. We'll go out to their house, have a quick peekaboo and that'll be it. We'll be in and out, Brussel sprout."

Her phrasing catches me off guard. "In and out so fast when they left a baby abandoned in a car? How long was he alone for?"

"Come on, Alex, you know the drill," she says, shaking her head. "You can't assume the kid is in danger just because some stranger said so. I need you there with me to fairly assess things, and we need proof of abuse or neglect."

Abuse or neglect. Suddenly I can't touch my latte. "How old is Buster?"

"Oh, a year at the most, I think." Minerva looks at me quizzically. "Are you okay?"

No, Minerva, I'm not okay, I want to say. As many cases as we resolve in child protection—kids living in horrible circumstances who we rescue and give a chance at a better life—new cases pop up at double the rate. I feel like Mickey Mouse in that old cartoon, the one we had to watch as kids at Christmas. Mickey's in his workshop, and it's flooding, and the mops are out of control and yet no matter how hard he tries, the water keeps pouring in, backing Mickey up the stairs. I hated that cartoon the first time I saw it, but it was always Ruth's favorite.

"Can we get going?" I stand up.

"Oh, alright then," she says, exhaling. "Although it wouldn't hurt to relaxez-vous for a minute. You'll be on stress leave in no time, just like everyone else, if you keep trying to save the world."

I ignore her and head for the door.

The Floyd property is on dilapidated farmland off of Highway 4. Minerva drives too fast out of town in our government vehicle. She has music playing on the Sirius radio like it's high summer and we're heading to the beach.

"Hey," she says, adjusting the rearview mirror, which has been nowhere near her line of vision the entire journey. "Have you seen Sully recently?"

"What?" I stare at her. Hooked around the front of me, my satchel feels like a shield.

"You know, Sully Mills? Handsome cop with the piercing eyes. Aren't you two buddies?"

I hate how she says the word "buddies," the way she separates the two syllables. Sully and I met a year ago through work. I guess you could say that we connected. I meet him for coffee at the Oven a couple of times a week. We're friends, not buddies. We're *just* friends.

"I don't see him that much." I tug at the seat belt cutting into my neck.

Minerva's eyebrows shift up for a second, but she doesn't say a word. I want to push her face with the full force of my hand.

A full minute or two later, she says, "He's single, right?"

What does it matter to her? "Do you want me to get you his number?" I ask in a monotone.

"*Get* me his number?" She bats at her bangs, fluffs and repositions them in the rearview mirror. "You mean *give* me his number. Because you have it already. And you text him all the time."

I shift in my seat. "I have a boyfriend, you know. Remember? The guy I live with?"

"Exactly! So share the wealth, sister." She smiles at me, then moves her eyes back to the road after swerving a little. The house is up ahead. She slows down, pulls into the driveway and jams the car into park. When we get out, we have to maneuver our way through clusters of shiny green goose shit that lead up a dirt track to the Floyd place. There's a fence and gate about a hundred meters from the house.

"Mr. and Mrs. Floyd were a gong show when I knew them," she says, turning, "but just so you know, they're the good gong show not the bad one. There's a difference."

"Is there?" How the hell can Minerva think drug addicts make good parents? We reach the gate, which has a sign on the front: BIG DOG BITES.

"That sign's been there since I was in Addictions. There was never a dog." She pulls at the gate, creating enough of a gap to squeeze through. A long stripe of mildew transfers to the front of her sweater. We walk up the potholed driveway together, past a bucket on its side and a couple of mismatched flip-flops.

"Oh, the house looks better," she says.

The home itself is squat and peeling, the deck ragged with rusted nails. On the porch outside the door is a cat litter tray full of crooked cigarette stubs. Next to that, a Hot Wheels car, blue, abandoned. If this is "better," then what on earth was the place like before?

She pauses on the top step of the deck. "Let's remember: even if Buster was left alone for a minute or two, when you're a mother, shit happens. You might not know that, but mothers do. Those of us with kids have all been there."

There's that card again, her favorite in the stack of superiority. I could retaliate, especially because I know about her son, know he's estranged and won't talk to her, but my heart's begun to race and my palms are sweating. The Hot Wheels car is faded and forlorn and reminds me of misery. Nothing good will come from this house. I wipe my hands on the back of my jeans.

"Okay, ready?" Minerva has her knuckles poised to knock, but the door is open. We walk into a tiny linoleum-floored vestibule that serves as some kind of pantry. Three shelves face us, empty apart from a couple of tins of baked beans, one of them opened with the ragged metal top sticking up. The glass of the main door itself is busted as if someone has put an elbow through it. Duct tape crisscrosses the pane.

"Let's get on with it," I say.

"Okay. If Frank Floyd comes at us, stay calm. In the old days, he was something of a charging bull."

I nod, wipe my palms once more on my pants. Nobody answers Minerva's knock, or the second one.

"Hello?" she calls out. "Anyone home?"

The vestibule smells musty, grainy, with the pungency that always comes with poverty. It's sour, hoppy, horrific. I cover my mouth with my sleeve. From inside we hear a crash and a shout, the sound of a plate clattering in a circle as it settles. Minerva pushes the rickety door open. She steps inside as Frank Floyd rounds the kitchen counter, leading with the top half of his body.

"I'm coming," he growls. He wears track pants, rolled at the waist, and a T-shirt that swamps him despite the fact that he's a huge guy. "Can't a man take a nap in his own house?" He spots Minerva, clearly recognizing her, "Oh, for fuck's sake. Here we go again. Send in the clowns."

"Mr. Floyd," Minerva says cheerily. "I hope you don't mind the intrusion."

"I do fucking mind, and I don't remember inviting you in."

I peep around Minerva, taking in Frank Floyd's bare feet, the ashtray on the floor, the dishes stacked up in the sink.

"We wanted to make sure everyone was okay in here. How are you doing today? I'm Minerva Cummins—do you remember me? We met years ago, but I've changed jobs since then: I'm here with Family Services. This is my co-worker, Alexandra Van Ness." Minerva sounds like she's gritting out a smile. I still have one hand on the door handle.

"No, no, *no*," Frank says, bashing his fist against his

own hip with each syllable like a toddler in a tantrum. "You're not coming in. You're trespassing. Nobody's fucking asked you to come here."

"It's okay, Frank. It's alright." She moves into the kitchen, both palms up. "Listen, I know you don't want us here. Is your wife around? Evelyn? Can we have a chat with her? We've just had a tiny little report and we need to check up on it."

I edge into the kitchen and stand close to Minerva. The house is as long and straight as a shipping container, the kitchen sprawling into the living room where, at the far end on a sofa with a missing cushion, a woman is sleeping facedown, wearing only an undershirt and panties. She sleeps as if dropped from a height, her limbs splayed. And it's then, only then that I see the baby.

He's tiny, sleeping bare-skinned, his face pressed dangerously against the cheap sponge of the couch cushion. He has nothing on but a diaper, the bulge of it round and tight like a soccer ball. The coloring of him, the tan and caramel skin tones, the way his hair sticks up at the crown, the bumpy little muscles in his shoulders—it all grips me like a fist. He's a carbon-copy. I have to rescue this child, just like I had to rescue another one before him.

"My wife's tired," Frank says, tracking my gaze. "She

banged her head." He's sweaty around the hairline, jerky in his movements.

"Should we call for an ambulance or bring her into the hospital?" I ask. Why isn't Minerva rushing toward the baby? He's clearly not safe. I take a step closer to the couch but tread on something that skids under my shoe. A cooked pasta tube squelches into the peeling floor tile.

"No! She didn't bang it that hard." Frank runs a mitt of fingers through greasy strands of his hair. "Look, everything's fine and shit. We're just tired. It's fucking difficult."

"Can we sit down, Frank?" Minerva asks. She pulls out a seat before he's responded and sits.

"What's difficult?" I say. "Is it something we can help you with?"

"Having a baby."

"Oh, steepest learning curve in the world!" Minerva says cheerfully. "I have a ten-year-old son and I couldn't tell you a thing about the first year of his life, Frank. It's literally a blur. You probably won't believe me, but I've been thinking lately that I wish I could do it all over again."

"Yeah," Frank says, uncertainly.

"Is Mrs. Floyd finding it really hard, too?" I ask.

"Yeah. I suppose. Yeah, yes. Look, okay, my wife didn't really bump her head."

"No? Then can we wake her up, do you think? It's really important that we speak with you both." I wait, still standing, while Minerva sits tidily amid the carnage that surrounds her.

"Yes, let's figure all of this out together." Minerva's arms rest on the table as if she's waiting for a Sunday roast. Has she seen the state of the house? Does she really think this is a safe environment for a child? Frank lumbers toward the sofa and pushes hard at his wife's shoulder. On the second attempt, she sits up, rubbing her eyes. Immediately she grabs Buster and he awakens, his face reddening, his arms sticking out straight, but he doesn't cry.

"The fuck are you two?" Evelyn looks from my face to Minerva's. "Who's this?"

"They're Family Services," Frank says, handing her a baggy pair of track pants he's found on the floor. "Put those on, and don't say shit."

Deep inside my stomach I feel the grit of pitted stone, the same gnawing that hits me every time I meet liars with a brand-new child.

Frank's sweating harder now, round circles visible in the armpits of his T-shirt. While Evelyn struggles to put on the pants without letting go of her son, Buster dips and flails.

"Mrs. Floyd, good morning," Minerva half-rises from her seat at the table, holding out a Family Services card that wavers pointlessly in the gap. "Do you re-member me? I'm Minerva Cummins and this is Alex Van Ness."

Evelyn doesn't look at either of us.

"We've had a report we need to follow up on."

"About what?" Evelyn sits, shifting Buster, who raises one little hand to hold onto the strap of her shirt.

Frank and I also take a seat at the table and the four of us face each other like opponents in a quiz show, Family Services versus the Floyds. Buster starts to wriggle.

"He needs a diaper change," I say quietly. "That one looks full."

"I'll get to it," Evelyn replies. "What do you want?" Buster makes strange little just-awake noises, a snuf-fling, more animal than infant. It's all I can do not to reach across and take him to my chest.

"We had a phone call," Minerva says.

"Who from?"

"It was anonymous. A woman called to say that you left little Buster unattended in a vehicle outside a pub-lic building."

Evelyn reaches back to the kitchen counter for a packet of cigarettes, tipping sideways on her chair so that the soft curve of Buster's forehead becomes visi-ble. That beautiful skin, olive and smooth. Evelyn pulls out a cigarette from the pack and lights it, jiggling the little boy in her lap as she smokes. She's bitten every fingernail she has, just like Ruth used to. I'm flooded again by all the lies, all the nervous little tremors and tics. They're universal among people hiding things.

"What do you mean unattended? What public building?"

"Well, a bystander noticed that Buster was in your car on his own with the engine running. You were in the post office. Does that ring a bell, Evelyn? It would have been yesterday, or possibly the day before."

"It wasn't me."

"I'm afraid the bystander wrote down your vehicle license number," Minerva says. We wait. Frank's shoulders slump. Thoughts flicker across Evelyn's face like she's assessing a poker hand.

"If it *was* me, I was only in the post office for two minutes."

"Two?" I say. "Are you sure?"

Frank elbows his wife suddenly, his voice cracked. "You fucking idiot. What the fuck were you thinking?"

"He was asleep!" Evelyn drags deeply on her cigarette and billows a long straight plume of smoke over Buster's head.

Minerva turns to me with a look that says, *I've got this.* But she hasn't. Meanwhile, Buster keeps reaching up to his mother's face, but each time she jerks her chin out of his way. *He wants you to look at him,* I think. *Why won't you?*

"He was fucking sleeping when I pulled up. Alright? I didn't want to wake him. I left the car running because otherwise the air-conditioning would shut off and it was the afternoon and hot. I'm not a fucking idiot."

"Totally. No. I get that," Minerva takes out a notebook, writes something and underlines it. "I'm a mother, too, Evelyn."

Evelyn rolls her eyes, but Minerva continues as though she hasn't seen. "I know how hard it can be to get things done with a little one in tow. But you can't leave Buster unattended. What if something happened? What if someone jumped in the car and just took off with him? You can't . . ." She searches for the most diplomatic phrasing. "Just, don't do that again, okay?"

"She won't," Frank mutters.

Evelyn lowers her head. I watch as ash droops on the end of her cigarette then falls to the floor. "Are you taking Buster away?" she asks flatly.

Oh, God, if only we could. The rules of procedure make it hard to remove a child. We need more evidence to present to court, but the second home visits are scheduled and never the same. The Floyds would have time to hide the drugs they're probably using.

Minerva knows this, too, so why isn't she being more proactive?

She snaps her notebook shut. "We're not taking Buster anywhere. Absolutely not. Do you know what I see?"

Abuse! I want to scream. *Neglect! A boy being thrown to the wolves!*

"I see two people trying very hard, two people who are nearing the end of their resources." Frank and Evelyn stare at her. "We're going to offer you some support services. Ways to make this whole thing a bit easier, so you're not"—she glances around at the debris of their house—"struggling so much. And we'll do a follow-up home visit. Just to see how you're getting on."

"Do we have to?" Frank asks. "Do we have to use the services? Do you have to come back?"

"Don't you want the help?" I ask, my eyes drilling into his.

He shrugs. So does his wife.

Minerva smiles like we've all just agreed on a fabulous business deal. "Great. So we'll head out now, but we'll be in touch soon once we organize some supports. You're doing very well. We'll just help you do a bit of a clean-up of Buster and . . . your home. And no more leaving him alone in the car."

"Alright," Evelyn says. "Al*right* already."

Minerva gets up. Is that it? She's the senior worker

here. Why is she not doing more of an inspection? Are we really going to leave the child in this filth?

Slowly I stand. "Could I just use the bathroom?" I ask. "You can lead me there. I won't go poking around."

Evelyn sighs. "I'll take her." Buster grips her neck as she stands. He's entirely devoid of language, a red flag in one-year-olds. We move down a skinny hallway toward the bathroom, Evelyn behind me. When I turn to look at her, her eyes are beady and granite-black. In a flash I'm back in my dream, those fingernails behind me, about to grab. Will she pull me to the ground like Ruth does? I swallow hard and we pass a bedroom that must be Buster's. Quickly I glance in. There's no furniture at all in the room apart from a standing bassinet. One stuffy lies on the floor—a blue bunny, the ears so sucked and slimy with grime that the fur looks like it's been pulled through an engine.

"Bathroom's this one," Evelyn tugs at my jacket and I jump. "Push harder," she says, doing so for me.

I go in and close the door behind me, moving a heavy black garbage bag away with my leg. There's no shower curtain, no soap. I breathe deeply with my eyes closed for a few seconds because my sister is *everywhere*.

There's a white bathroom cabinet over the sink, and I pull open the smudged front of it, rattling among lidless Tylenol bottles and brown-tinged Q-tips for some clear evidence of a drug habit. There's nothing. They're hiding it elsewhere. *Goddamn it*, I think.

I flush the toilet, or try to, my jacket sleeve low over my fingers. Back out in the corridor, Evelyn is waiting for me, bouncing her son. We walk in silence to the door, where Minerva is standing with Frank.

"All set?" Minerva asks. She's working herself up to a chipper goodbye and makes another attempt to hand over her business card. "So we'll be in touch. The future is bright. Don't worry: we'll work on all of this as a team."

Neither of the Floyds take her business card. She sets it on the counter.

"Please call if you need immediate help or assistance," Minerva waves as she backs away down the porch steps. We leave them both there in the doorway, Buster obscured by the sinewy arms of his mom.

In the car, Minerva turns to me. "That went well." She snatches at levers on each side of the steering wheel, trying to find the left signal.

"What?"

"That whole visit. Didn't you think? They're doing so much better. I feel we can help them."

She's out of her mind. If she thinks Buster is safe in that environment, she's nothing but another risk factor in his life. "Minerva, their house was awful. That smell?"

"What smell?" She turns the car around, making traffic slow as she swerves into the right-hand lane.

"Like old beer. Like grain at harvest." I shudder.

"Haven't you got used to that yet?" she asks.

"No, and I don't want to. How are you okay with the situation that child is in? There were definite signs of neglect."

"Be careful with that term," she says quickly. "Just because the Floyds are struggling doesn't mean they don't love their son, or can't look after him. They need some scaffolds around them."

I find my fingers clenching and jam them under my thighs. Minerva might have more years on the job than I do, but in all that time she hasn't figured out that Child Protection is an oxymoron. Even when we save kids or remove them, workers like her throw them back into the fray. *Safe enough* is her motto, but it isn't mine. We drive too fast in silence.

After a while, I can't help myself. "They don't even change his diapers!" I say. "I bet he has welts all over his backside if we'd bothered to look." I know I sound petulant, but I don't care. Because I'm the one doing my job properly. I'm trying to protect a child.

"You know the rules. There were no grounds for removal, Alex. They weren't high on drugs. Which incidentally I'm very proud about. And there were no signs of abuse. They just seem overwhelmed." Her hands whiten at the knuckle where she grips the steering wheel. "Loving someone and protecting them aren't always the same thing."

Enabler. She wills herself to see the best in people because she can't handle conflict. And she won't admit the impotence that we real child protection workers feel when we have to obey the fucking "rules"—which serve no one, especially not the children whose needs aren't being met. She sets the bar so low and refuses to see it. I stare out the window and say nothing.

The rest of the day passes at the steady pace of paperwork and doleful phone calls. I have more than twenty files on my caseload, some of them reported incidents, others active investigations. That's a whole crowd of children I'm desperately trying to save. As I sift through the voicemails left on my machine—most of them from bio parents, a lot of them incoherent or hateful—I think about all the gates I'm guarding for these kids and how none of them really know it's me.

By four o'clock, I'm happy to start the walk home to the loft. When I step inside the apartment, I see Chase standing in boxers and a yellow shirt with the collar up, dicing tomatoes. He turns when he hears me.

"Hey, beautiful," he says, the paring knife still in his hand. In the living room the baseball game is on, scores from around the league zooming across the screen in ticker tape. "Everything okay?"

He always asks me that. But how can *everything* be okay? To be fair, he hasn't seen what I've seen today. He doesn't know what I know. The bulge of Buster's diaper. The press of his small face into the couch cushion. The utter apathy of his parents. Chase's world is much brighter than that. It's a good thing. And his brightness buoys me. It's what I love most about him.

I smile. "Most things are fine."

"Tough day?" He rinses his hands and then grabs me a wineglass from the cupboard, fetches a chilled bottle of white from the fridge. "I don't know how you do it. You could have gotten a job in a coffee shop, you know. Just deal with caffeinating people all day."

I laugh a little every time he makes suggestions like this, although I'm not sure he's actually joking.

"How was your day?" I sit on the chrome bar stool at the kitchen counter and pry off my sneakers, letting each one drop with a thud. "You got in late last night. How was the photoshoot? Where did you go again?" Chase is in marketing for our local ski hill, Powderkeg. More often than not, he's the face of all the promotional advertising—the billboards, the website, the commercials—but I can never keep up with which West Coast ski resort he's filming in, or when. Most of his work is November through April, but there's always the odd shoot in the summer months to preempt the new season. It's nice to have him around more at this time of year, though. He helps a lot with meal planning.

"We just did some promo shots for next year." He inspects the wine bottle, vaguely. "Inside-outside stuff in Breckenridge. They turned out great. They took a lot of head and shoulders shots of me and the director was really happy."

"Of course he was. Are you going away again over the summer?"

"No, that should be it now." Chase cracks the wine and pours a generous portion, sliding the glass across to me. "Downtime."

"Good," I say. "I miss you when you're gone."

He reaches across the countertop to hold my hand but I withdraw it—I haven't had a chance to wash properly yet. If I told him what I'd touched today, he'd be horrified. His smile falters. "Are you hungry?"

I shake my head. "I have to take a shower first. I have to get this day off my skin."

"Oh," he says. There's a second where I imagine him taking the expensive wineglass back. "I've made a new turkey and quinoa dish. It's paleo. Full of good proteins. But we can hold off. We can eat in, say, twenty or so." He picks up his knife and begins dicing again, the knife easily severing the tomato's skin.

"That'd be great." I take a sip of the crisp wine, then slide off the stool. In the bathroom, I peel off my clothes. Social work makes me want to scrub my entire body with a wire brush every day. I wonder for a moment if Sully feels that way about his job, too. After a quick shower, I head back out, toweling my hair as I enter the kitchen. Through the open bay windows, a chickadee is singing its binary song in the street. That's when I hear a knock at the door. Chase, tea towel over one shoulder, pauses his chopping.

"Are you expecting someone?"

"No, definitely not."

I wrap the towel around my neck, then head to the front door and pull it open. I see a face more than anything, the paleness of it stark against dark hair. Long hair, familiar. Blue, damaged eyes. Immediately, I feel my knees might give out, like I might fall to the ground. I cover my mouth with both hands and stare.

It's her. It's Ruth Van Ness. My sister.

OUT TO WORK